Icespell

C. J. Busby

Illustrated by David Wyatt

Scholastic Canada Ltd.
Toronto New York London Auckland Sydney
Mexico City New Delhi Hong Kong Buenos Aires

For Philip, who always laughs at the right bits

Scholastic Canada Ltd.
604 King Street West, Toronto, Ontario M5V 1E1, Canada

Scholastic Inc.
557 Broadway, New York, NY 10012, USA

Scholastic Australia Pty Limited
PO Box 579, Gosford, NSW 2250, Australia

Scholastic New Zealand Limited
Private Bag 94407, Botany, Manukau 2163, New Zealand

Scholastic Children's Books
Euston House, 24 Eversholt Street, London NW1 1DB, UK

www.scholastic.ca

Library and Archives Canada Cataloguing in Publication
Busby, Cecilia, 1966-
Icespell / by C.J. Busby ; illustrated by David Wyatt.
(Frogspell ; 3)
ISBN 978-1-4431-2479-9
I. Wyatt, David, 1968- II. Title. III. Series: Busby,
Cecilia, 1966- . Frogspell ; 3.
PZ7.B96Ic 2013   j823'.92   C2012-908476-X

Text copyright © 2012 by C.J. Busby.
Illustrations copyright © 2012 by David Wyatt

Published by arrangement with Templar Publishing Ltd.
This edition published in Canada by Scholastic Canada Ltd. in 2014.

6 5 4 3 2 1   Printed in Great Britain CP 149   14 15 16 17 18

MIX
Paper from
responsible sources
FSC® C020471

Contents

An Enemy
in the Armoury

There was something lurking in the darkness at the far end of the armoury.

Max froze. His hand just inches away from his sword, he peered into the gloom, trying to see beyond the shadows. He could have sworn he'd heard a scuffle, seen a gleam of movement. But now everything was still, and the only sounds were the distant clash of swords in the practice yard and Sir Gareth shouting at the novice squires.

Most of Camelot was out in the sunshine, enjoying a chance to get some swordplay in before the Annual Festival of Chivalry, which started in three weeks. Max had been sent in to fetch a spare target for archery practice — but they were stored right at the back of the armoury. In the shadows.

Max started to move forward slowly and carefully, his hand on his sword, trying to look like he was ready to fight. In reality, his sword skills were not renowned, and he was pretty sure he'd come off worse against anything except a stray chicken. Or possibly a frog.

"Wh— who's there?" he called into the darkness, trying to keep his voice level but not really succeeding. He could see a darker shape within the grey of the shadows — a rather tall and menacing shape. Definitely not a chicken. Max drew his sword, then took a swift step backwards as the shape rose up out of the shadows and launched itself toward him with a roar. Max toppled over a pile of armour and fell sprawling onto the ground, his sword clattering across the room.

He looked up to see that the dark shape was actually a tall, thin boy with a dark tunic and spiky black hair, who was now standing over him and laughing.

"Well, well, Pendragon. Glad to see you're as clumsy and pathetic as ever. Merlin might be teaching you magic, but he obviously can't do anything about the fact that you're a hopeless loser."

Max scrambled to his feet, but the boy had already sidestepped him and was on his way out of the armoury, still laughing.

"Eat dung, Snotty!" Max yelled after him, but if the boy heard, he made no sign. Max clenched his fists. Adrian Hogsbottom, better known as Snotty, was his worst enemy. Ever since they'd first met, they'd hated each other — and the rivalry had got worse since Snotty and his father had started plotting against King Arthur with Lady Morgana le Fay. Max shivered just thinking about Morgana —

the kingdom's most powerful sorceress. He and his sister Olivia had helped foil two of Morgana's plots to bring down her half-brother, the king, and make herself queen in his place. Max was pretty sure it was only thanks to Merlin's protection that he was not at this moment a piece of oozy slime at the bottom of the kingdom's biggest manure heap.

Thinking of Morgana's plots made Max narrow his eyes. What exactly had Snotty been doing, lurking at the back of the armoury? As far as Max knew, there were only archery targets down here, plus a few piles of broken armour and swords waiting to be mended. There was no reason for Snotty to be anywhere near the place.

Max dragged out the target he needed, and then had a good look around, under the benches and behind the piles of rusty shields and broken lances. He even balanced on an old trestle table to see if there was anything up on the shelves that ran round the top of the room, but everything seemed undisturbed, still covered in layers of old dust. He shrugged. Whatever it was, it looked like Snotty had been interrupted before he could do anything.

Max picked up the target and headed off into the sunlight. Behind him, the room settled back into silence. Deep in the shadows, hidden from view by an old rusty bucket, lay a small pile of glittering white powder that Max would instantly have recognized as a spell. Nestling in the centre of the pile was a small jagged chip of grey flint. It was placed carefully next to the easternmost wall of the armoury, and hence in the absolute easternmost corner of Castle Camelot.

***

Thud!

Olivia's arrow hit the centre of the target and stayed there, quivering. It was her third bullseye.

"Hurrah! Well done! Right in the red bit!" cried Adolphus, Olivia's pet dragon, who was bouncing around the target, waving his blue-green forked tail, flapping his wings and generally making a nuisance of himself, as usual.

"Show off," muttered Max, as he headed off to retrieve the arrows. His own were rather less impressively scattered around the edges of the target. One was buried in the trunk of an old beech tree several feet away.

"Just a bit off target, that one," observed Max's pet rat, Ferocious, poking his head out of Max's tunic and surveying the scattered arrows. "Remind me never to get within a hundred feet of anything you're aiming at, Max."

"Yes, yes, very funny," said Max, wrenching the arrow out of the tree and trudging back to Olivia. "I don't see why I still have to do stupid target practice anyway. I'm going to be a wizard, not a knight."

"Well, you know what Father told you," said Olivia. "You *still* have to have basic knight training. Even wizards need to use a sword sometimes."

Max grimaced. Their father, Sir Bertram Pendragon, was every inch a knight, from the tips of his magnificent moustache to the toes of his oversized feet. He was as strong as an ox, surprisingly nifty with his sword and renowned throughout the kingdom as the Knight Who Can Quaff the Most Grog in a Single Swallow. Max, on the other hand, was slight for his eleven years, with untidy brown hair, a singular lack of coordination and a healthy fear of horses. He was pretty sure all the knightly skills in the family had been passed on to his sister. Although she was two years younger and hadn't had much training, Olivia was already a better rider, considerably better at archery and was fast becoming better at swordplay, too.

Max threw himself down on the grass and stretched out in the sunshine.

"That's it. I've had enough of archery, I've had enough of whacking the dummy with a lance and I've definitely had enough of sword practice. My shoulder hurts."

Olivia plonked herself down next to him.

"You do realize I've only got three weeks left till the Festival of Chivalry, Max? You promised to help me train."

Max groaned. Olivia was entered for the Squire's Challenge, the most prestigious competition for novice squires in the kingdom. Normally she wouldn't even have been allowed to enter, being a girl, but she had nagged Sir Bertram mercilessly till he gave her permission, and King Arthur had bent the rules to let her have a try. If she won, Sir Bertram had promised she could train to be a knight. He had been pretty certain he wouldn't have to keep his promise — all the best squires in the kingdom would be competing, and Olivia had only been training for a few months.

Max, however, thought she had quite a good chance. His younger sister was quite ruthless when it came to fighting, and she was a fearless rider. What she lacked in training, she more than made up for in cunning and brute force.

"Sorry," he said, not sounding sorry at all. "Can't help. Got a lesson with Merlin."

Just saying this made him feel six inches taller. He might not be very skilled with a sword, but Max did have quite a talent for magic — and now he had

Merlin himself to teach him. Merlin was the most powerful wizard in the kingdom, but he looked like any other of King Arthur's many knights, with dark plain clothes and a long sword buckled to his belt — until you caught a glance from his bright hawk-like eyes and felt the power behind them.

Max had been having lessons with Merlin for the past few weeks, and he was buzzing with all the magic he'd tried and the spells he'd learned.

"Are you going to tell him about Snotty?" asked Olivia. Max had told the others about his encounter with his worst enemy. All of them had experienced Snotty's plotting before, and they were all highly suspicious.

"That boy is definitely up to something, mark my words," said Ferocious darkly. "We need to let Merlin know."

"But I couldn't see anything," said Max. "I think I probably disturbed him before he could do whatever it was he was planning. I don't know if it's even worth mentioning."

Olivia grimaced. "He's a poisonous toadwart, and if he was lurking in the armoury, then odds are he was about to do something foul. Morgana's going to be here for the Festival of Chivalry — I bet they're planning something."

Max nodded. "We need to keep an eye on Snotty. I'm sure he is up to something. But there's a week before Morgana gets here, and nothing's going to happen till then."

But Max was wrong. Something quite spectacular *was* going to happen. And when it did, it would be all his fault.

Merlin's Magic

Merlin's chambers were simple and plainly furnished, with a long, narrow window looking out onto the moat. Max stood at the window, looking down at the greenish water. It seemed hardly any time since the day he'd been transformed into a frog in this same room, and Snotty Hogsbottom had dangled him out of the window before casually dropping him fifty feet down to the moat below.

Max shivered, remembering the killer pike that was probably still down there looking for tasty frogs to swallow whole.

The heavy oak door to the chamber flew open and Merlin strode in, pulling off his long dark travelling cloak and unbuckling his sword.

"Sorry, Max, I didn't mean to be late. We had a bit of an alarm call down in the south, and I went to investigate. Everyone's a bit jumpy these days, with all these rumours of an enemy sorceress."

He winked, and Max grinned. Merlin was well aware that the recent plots against the king were the work of Morgana le Fay, but she'd managed to make sure she had an alibi each time, and King Arthur was very reluctant to accuse his half-sister. Instead, the story was that some "unknown sorceress" had been behind the plots.

"Right," said Merlin, rubbing his hands. "Time for some magic."

Max felt the familiar thrill of lessons with Merlin. He never knew what would happen next, and he was constantly surprised by what he could do. Spells for seeing from afar, spells for linking one bit of magic to another, spells for detecting other spells. But today, something even more unusual was clearly in store, because instead of being down in the cellars, with the cauldrons and spell ingredients, they were in Merlin's rooms, and there was no magical apparatus ready at all.

Merlin smiled, his eyes bright in his weathered face.

"Today," he said solemnly, "we are going to do magic without any potions or spells."

Max looked at him, rather taken aback. He'd never even *heard* of magic without spells or potions. Everyone did magic with potions. You took ingredients, you put them in a cauldron, you said the right words — and there was your spell. You could make it work at once, or embed it in an object, or keep it in the form of a powder or a liquid, to use another time. Even when witches or wizards looked like they weren't using a potion, there was always one somewhere, a sprinkle of dust on their hands, a droplet of spell on their fingers. It was why they went around with huge numbers of pouches and bags and bottles attached to their belts or secreted in their clothes. You never knew what spell you might need at short notice.

But Merlin was different. Merlin looked like a knight, not a wizard, and suddenly Max realized why that was. It was precisely because he *didn't* have the usual clattering collection of potion bottles and packets of powder tucked into belt pouches or hanging around his neck, bulking out his clothes. He looked like a lean, plain, simple knight — no tricks. Yet Max had seen his magic, knew he could remove spells with a twitch of his finger. Why had he never thought about how odd that was before?

Merlin smiled as he saw Max's dawning realization.

"That's right, Max. No potions. No powders. Interesting, isn't it?"

"But how . . ." said Max, bewildered.

Merlin beckoned him over to a table near the window, and they both sat down.

"Max — have you ever wondered how you made a spell for turning people into frogs when no one else except me had ever done it before?"

"It was an accident," said Max. "Olivia knocked a jar of bat's-squeak-breath off the shelf and it ended up in my spell by mistake."

Merlin laughed. "It was a mistake, yes — but I'm betting that just when that extra ingredient landed in the cauldron you were thinking about frogs."

Max frowned. He *had* been thinking about frogs. He'd been thinking about what a nuisance Olivia was and how, if only it were possible, he'd turn her into a frog and dump her in the castle duckpond. When the spell had done exactly that to all of them — him, Olivia *and* Ferocious — Max had thought it must have been just a coincidence.

"No such thing as coincidence," said Merlin cheerfully, when Max suggested this. "The spell turned you into frogs because you yourself added the final twist of necessary magic — and it's distinctly possible that it was that same magic that meant it was the jar of bat's-squeak-breath and not a jar of, say, earwig hair, that ended up in the cauldron."

Max frowned. He found it hard to believe that he'd made the spell happen by thinking the magic into place.

"But lots of people must have *thought* about making a frogspell before. Why did it work for me?"

Merlin looked at him thoughtfully. "It's a good question, Max. But it's not just thinking about it that's important. It's the ability to turn that thought into an extra part of the spell. For animal transformations, it's quite essential — it's why most people can't do them, however powerful a witch or wizard they might be. Morgana, for example, is extremely skilled with cauldron spells and can bind together very powerful magics — but she can't make any magic happen simply by thinking it into existence. Very few people can. I am one of them. I think it is highly likely that you are another."

Max swallowed. He was pretty sure that Merlin was overestimating his ability with magic. His frogspell had been impressive, but that had just been luck. Nothing else he'd ever done had been out of the ordinary — apart from the odd spectacular mistake. Maybe this was where he'd get found out and sent home in disgrace.

Merlin put a small silver bowl on the table in front of them.

"Now, Max. Think of the invisibility potion we brewed a few days ago. Think of the shape of the magic, once it was made. Then gather that feeling of the magic in your mind and cast it onto the bowl. Make it disappear!"

Max took a deep breath and stared at the bowl.

He clenched his fists, and screwed up his eyes, and willed it to disappear ...

He shut his eyes even tighter, muttered, "Disappear!" and opened his eyes again ...

He opened them extra wide and goggled at the

bowl, he stuck his tongue out and turned red with the effort of willing it away . . .

After five minutes, the bowl still looked exactly as it had at the beginning, not even a hint of a haze of invisibility.

Merlin watched Max's efforts solemnly, but his mouth twitched at the corner.

"Perhaps we need a . . . ahem . . . practical demonstration first," he said, in a kindly voice. "Come with me, Max, and we'll go down to the moat."

The moat was looking particularly green and murky, with tendrils of weeds floating on the surface. Max looked at it doubtfully.

"You have been a frog quite a few times now, Max," Merlin said cheerfully. "I think you'll find you can feel your way into that transformation, with a little help from me."

Max was pretty sure he couldn't. He was pretty sure he was only minutes away from being sent home as a fraud. There was no way he could do a frogspell transformation without any frogspell.

Merlin put his hand on Max's shoulder.

"Think, Max, of the shape of the spell, and the feeling of being a frog. Think of the buzz of the magic as it hits you. Think of the shiver of the change from human to frog ... And let that magic *flow*."

As he said the last words, Max could feel a tingle of magic from Merlin's hand. He felt it spread, and a tide of answering magic rising from somewhere deep inside himself. Then, like the rush of water from an upturned bucket, he felt suddenly drenched in magic and he slipped head first into the moat.

***

The water was dim and green but felt quite pleasant. This was almost certainly because Max was now a frog. A frog! Without a frogspell potion! He had done it, all by himself!

Well, not quite. Max remembered the tingle of magic from Merlin's hand — but also the answering rush of magic that was clearly his own. Now he thought about it, he'd always known that magic was there — but never realized it could be used like that. He still wasn't sure he *could* use it without Merlin's help. But at least he had a much better sense of how to try.

Max kicked his back legs and cruised through the murky water, enjoying the feel of it on his skin, blowing a few bubbles that floated upwards like silvery balloons and burst on the surface. Suddenly he noticed a large fish keeping pace with him, a long elegant grey carp with whiskers and an amused expression. It looked rather like . . .

"Merlin! Is that you?"

"Indeed it is. It's a long time since I've swum in the moat — I'd forgotten how pleasant and cool it is. And how little effort swimming takes when you've got a tail." And Merlin twitched his expertly and shot forward into the gloom.

"Hey! Wait for me!" called Max, and tried to catch up with him, but frogs are not quite as streamlined as fish, and however fast Max swam, the dark bulky shape of the carp was always just ahead.

Until it stopped, and half turned, and Max almost shot into its gaping mouth.

At which point he realized that he had not been following the carp. He had been following a pike. A very large and fierce-looking pike. In fact, quite possibly the very same pike that had nearly eaten Max a few months earlier.

Danger in the Moat!

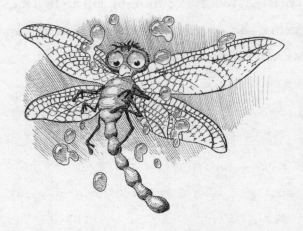

The pike snapped its jaws shut like a steel trap, but Max dodged the razor-sharp teeth and shot upward as fast as he could. His only thought was to get back onto dry land as quickly as possible. He leaped out of the water, the pike only just behind him, snapping angrily. The bank was still a few feet away, and Max was clearly going to drop back into the water, just where the giant fish would be waiting hungrily.

A dragonfly buzzed past Max, hovering over the surface of the water, and in that instant he mentally grabbed great handfuls of the magic he knew was inside him and flung it at the dragonfly, at himself, at the moat, and at the pike. He wasn't quite sure what he was trying to achieve but it had a lot to do with not falling back down into the water and the pike's waiting jaws.

WHOOSH!

There was a buzzing and a burst of light, and suddenly everything around Max seemed to be turning over and over in a dizzy whirl of bank, water and sky. Max felt giddy, and slightly sick, and wasn't at all sure where he'd ended up. He didn't seem to be inside the pike at least, because he could see the sunlight glinting on motes of dust and reflecting off the water...

Suddenly Max realized where he was. He was in the air, above the moat, and he had turned himself into a dragonfly. The giddiness came from the speed at which he was flying and a constant change of direction as he slightly overdid a wingbeat on one side or the other. Gradually he managed to bring his flying under control, and to keep the surface of the water more or less steady underneath him. He flew up a little higher from the surface, safely out of the reach of any jumping fish, and started to enjoy speeding along in a straight line.

"I did it!" he thought. "I did magic without any potions! I turned myself into a dragonfly!"

He was so triumphant at having managed such an amazing piece of magic on his own, that at first he didn't notice he was heading straight for the wall of the castle. By the time he did, it was too late. There was only one option, and Max took it. He flapped desperately to the left, and whizzed straight through a dark narrow window into a small chamber.

The moment he was in the room, Max realized there were people in there, too. One of them raised a hand to swat him, and he dived sideways, coming to a quivering rest on a tapestry along one wall. Luckily the tapestry was brightly coloured, and

Max disappeared nicely into the pattern. It seemed like a good place to hide while he assessed the situation.

Max peered at the people in the room. They looked vaguely familiar, although dragonfly vision took a bit of getting used to. Then he heard one of them speak, and he knew instantly who they were.

"Get your fat head out of the way, Jerome. I need to find a good hiding place, and it's got to be on this side because this is the northernmost wall of the castle."

Max would have known that sneering voice anywhere. Which meant the other figure must be Snotty's usual sidekick, Jerome Stodmarsh, a stocky boy with red hair and a face like a pug. What were they up to?

He fluttered a little closer, trying hard not to draw attention to himself. Just where they were huddled together, there was an ornately carved chest. Max settled on it and kept as still as he could. As he watched, Snotty placed a small pile of white powder on the ground behind the chest, right next to the wall. In the centre of the white powder he placed a small jagged piece of grey stone. Then both figures stood up, and Snotty dusted off his hands.

"There. That's the last one. Come on, Jerome, let's go and whack a few novices in the practice yard . . ."

They left, and the heavy oak door of the chamber crashed shut behind them. Which meant Max would have to get back out through the narrow slit window.

Max had often watched flies and other insects trying to get out of a small window and thought they were ridiculously stupid. Now he wished he had been more charitable. Not only was dragonfly vision not quite as sharp as he'd hoped, it was also very difficult to judge speed and angles to get exactly where he was aiming for. Max lost count of the times he found himself dazed on the window ledge, having knocked himself out flying into the wall. Finally, he narrowed his eyes and aimed ever so slightly to the left of the window. Mentally

crossing his fingers, he flew directly at the wall ...
and emerged into the sunlight on the other side,
breathing a sigh of relief.

But his relief did not last long. Because, try as
Max might, he could not see Merlin anywhere, either
in the moat or beside it. In fact, there didn't appear to
be anyone around at all. The moat was as still as a
pond, the sun was shining fiercely, and most people
had retreated indoors for a midday meal or a quiet
nap. Even when he managed to find the gatehouse and
fly through it, the castle yard beyond was deserted.

He settled on a stone buttress, folded his
shimmering wings, and considered the situation. He
was a dragonfly. No one knew he was a dragonfly,
not even Merlin, who had last seen him as a frog. If
Max didn't want to end up as a dragonfly for the rest
of his life, he was going to have to find some way of
reactivating the magic he knew was inside him to
turn himself back.

Max concentrated hard and thought about being
a boy. He thought about the handfuls of magic he'd

flung at the pike in his terror. He thought about the feeling of being drenched in magic, the feeling of being transformed into another creature. He held his breath and *willed* as hard as he could to be a boy.

But he was still a dragonfly.

Max closed his eyes and tried again. He willed it so hard he thought his dragonfly brain would burst. He flapped his wings and shouted random spell words in the hope that it might get something started. But nothing happened.

Slugs' eyeballs! This was getting serious. It looked like he might be destined to stay a dragonfly forever. But then his antennae pricked up. Max heard a clash of sword on metal, and a distinctly familiar voice.

"Ow! Dungballs! I've whacked my knee *again*!"

Just around the corner, a small but sturdy figure with short, messy brown hair was picking up her sword from the ground and preparing to do battle again with a rusty old practice dummy. Max remembered spending hours trying to disarm a similar dummy at Castle Perilous. There was a trick to hooking the dummy's sword out of its metal hand — but get it wrong, and you might find yourself slicing your own leg off instead. From the look of Adolphus, who had one claw over his eyes, wincing, Olivia had not had much luck this session.

Max flew across and landed on Olivia's shoulder, as close to her ear as he could get. Ever since they'd both been transformed into frogs, a few months before, they'd been able to understand animal speech. But just as Max prepared to shout as loud as he could into her ear, Olivia's hand came up automatically and brushed him off. Max went tumbling through the air, turned three somersaults and landed on the ground, feeling extremely dazed.

The world took a few seconds to stop whirling around and around. When it did, Max realized he was looking straight into the eyes of Adolphus the dragon. Adolphus, the dimmest dragon in the kingdom. Adolphus, who generally ate first and asked questions later.

Adolphus had just started to open his mouth when Max, shouting as loud as he possibly could, bellowed, "No! Stop! It's me — Max!"

Adolphus stopped and peered at the dragonfly in front of him.

"I beg your pardon?" he said.

"It's me — Max! It's Max! Tell Olivia!" shouted Max, hopping up and down and flapping his wings madly.

Adolphus looked puzzled. He frowned in concentration. He took a deep breath. He scratched his ear with his back leg. Then he looked down at the dragonfly again.

"Did you say you knew Max?"

"No," said Max, thankful that at least he was having a conversation, rather than being digested. "I *am* Max. It's Max! Tell Olivia!"

"Umm, OK," said Adolphus doubtfully, and called out to Olivia. "Er ... there's a dragonfly here. He's called Max. Funny — same name as our Max. Anyway. He wants to talk to you, for some reason."

Olivia stopped in the middle of a complicated manoeuvre, and frowned.

"Says his name is Max? That's an odd name for a dragonfly ... Are you sure?"

"Well, umm, I think so," said Adolphus uncertainly. "Maybe you'd better talk to him."

Olivia came over and bent down. She put out her finger and Max crawled onto it, clinging tightly as she raised him up to her face.

"So," she said. "You're called Max."

"I *am* Max, idiot!" he shouted in his tiny dragonfly voice. "It's me! I turned myself into a dragonfly and now I can't turn myself back. Have we got any antidote?"

Olivia looked at Max and started to laugh. In fact, she couldn't stop laughing. She had to put him down on the ground so she could really howl with laughter.

Max rolled his eyes and waited for her to reach the hiccupping stage. Then he took off, landed on the end of her nose and demanded the antidote, that second, or he would never help her train again.

"Sorry," she said, wiping her eyes. "But I don't think we have any left. I'll have to . . . kiss you." Which sent her off into another fit.

Eventually, she lifted Max up on her finger and kissed the tip of one wing, which he held out very gingerly.

WHOOSH!

There were stars, and Max landed with a thud on the ground, fully human again. Adolphus bounced around joyfully, quite amazed to see him, and told Max what a shame it was that he'd missed the chance to meet a dragonfly that had the same name.

At that moment Merlin came striding into the yard with Ferocious on his shoulder. He gave a shout of relief.

"Max! Thank goodness! I thought I felt transformation magic taking place. Everything all right? Where did you go?"

Max explained about being a dragonfly, and Merlin apologized for not getting to him sooner, when he'd realized Max had started following the pike.

"When I did get there, I was just about to whip you out of the way when you came up with that blast of magic. Gave me a bit of trouble," said Merlin, gingerly feeling his nose. "Quite some power you've got there Max, once you learn to control it. I don't suppose you managed to turn yourself back?"

Max shook his head.

"Never mind, never mind, early days . . . Where did you go, anyway? I lost track of you while I was trying to deal with almost having my nose broken."

Max told Merlin and the others about seeing Snotty and Jerome, but he had got so dizzy and disoriented as a dragonfly, that he had no idea which chamber he'd been in. As Max described the white powder, Merlin frowned, and a strange, absent expression came over his face, like he was trying hard to detect a faint smell. After a few moments, he looked around at them all.

"They've been planting a spell of some kind. I've

tried to sense where, but I can't. I rather suspect that the white powder contains some kind of shielding magic that's hiding it from me. And if it's good enough to stop me, then there's really only one person in the kingdom who could have made it."

Merlin looked fierce, and Max shivered. Lady Morgana le Fay. So Snotty was up to something, and it *did* have something to do with Morgana. He told Merlin about finding Snotty in the armoury that morning.

"So. Maybe that was his first attempt, and now he's managed to plant the spell somewhere else. We'll have to see if we can find out where ... But in the meantime, keep an eye out, all of you. We are almost certainly going to have some trouble from Morgana at the Festival of Chivalry, and we need to be ready."

Icespell

The black knight stood motionless, square on his huge black charger, his lance extended in front of him. Olivia took a deep breath, steadied her horse, and took a firm grip of her lance. She narrowed her eyes, sighting along the lance at the brooding knight, and then nudged the horse into a trot.

"Go, Olivia!" shouted Max from the stands, and Adolphus, who was sitting beside him, waved his forked tail and snorted a small spout of flame. Olivia frowned. It was bad enough being the only girl doing the training for the Squire's Challenge, without having embarrassing family members cheering for you. But there was worse to come. As she headed at a canter toward the waiting knight, the unmistakable bellow of Sir Bertram Pendragon's hearty voice rang out across the jousting ground.

"Whack him one, Olivia! That's my girl!"

Olivia rolled her eyes, then grasped her lance firmly and focused on the knight in front of her. There were two dangers to avoid at all costs. One, being hit by the knight's lance on any part of your body, and two, hitting him anywhere on his left-hand side. The ideal option was to get him straight between the eyes, and this Olivia fully intended to do.

She avoided his lance in style, by leaning over in the saddle just a fraction to the left, and then she struck in her turn. Unfortunately, her lance wavered at the last second, and she caught the knight on his left shoulder. The flat iron figure spun around smartly and his lance whacked her hard on the back as she galloped past.

There was an outbreak of cheering from the other end of the jousting ground, and Olivia, smarting from the blow and from annoyance at missing, ground her teeth. Of course, the biggest cheer of all came from the red-haired Mordred, son of King Lot of Orkney and her biggest rival.

"Slimy, good-for-nothing son of a septic carbuncle," she muttered, as she led her horse slowly back down to where the other squires were gathered. "I'd like to see you do better!"

But to Olivia's ire, Mordred, who was next, managed to place his lance perfectly. The great iron knight toppled over backwards and crashed to the ground with a resounding clang. Mordred waved his lance in the air triumphantly, and all the novices clapped. All except Olivia.

"Never mind, my dear, can't expect to beat the son of the King of Orkney, eh?" said Sir Bertram, patting her heartily on the back. "He's been training since he was five years old. You're very good, you know, but you can't expect miracles."

Secretly, Sir Bertram was rather relieved to see that Olivia had a serious rival. He'd been very much afraid she might actually pull it off, might win the Squire's Challenge. And although it would be rather a triumph in some ways, it *would* mean he'd have to keep his word and let her train to be a knight, and his wife, Lady Griselda, would never let him hear the end of it. He stroked his magnificent moustache and tried not to look too pleased.

"Well, now, afternoon off, eh? You should go down to the river with Max. Got to stick around in the castle, myself. The king's calling a meeting of all his knights, see what we can do about this blasted sorceress causing trouble. Otherwise I'd come with you — lovely day for a swim!"

"Yes, hurrah, let's go to the river!" said Adolphus, bounding up to them and flapping his wings. "I love swimming!"

Olivia sighed. She only had three weeks left to

get good enough at the mock joust to beat Mordred, and she would rather have spent the afternoon tilting at the practice dummy. But Sir Bertram was right, it was a lovely afternoon, and maybe some time off would do her good. And of course, she could always try out a few sword manoeuvres on Max. She brightened, and nodded, and Sir Bertram clapped her on the shoulder.

"Excellent! Don't be back late — supper in the Great Hall tonight. Caradoc's just returned from his travels, has a new song for us all."

Olivia exchanged glances with Max and they both grinned. "Caradoc" the bard had been quite an ally in their last adventure. But what Sir Bertram didn't know was that Caradoc's name was actually Lancelot, and he *wasn't* actually a bard. He was really a knight, but because he was working as a spy for Merlin, he had to keep his knightly skills a secret. He was also pretty good at magic, although he kept that talent a secret, too — Lady Morgana and her fellow plotters wouldn't be suspicious of a lowly bard, and that was the way Merlin wanted things to stay.

Max and Olivia were looking forward to seeing Lancelot again, and maybe he'd have some news about just what Morgana was plotting for the festival.

***

"Ow!" Max's sword tumbled through the air and landed with a clatter among the rocks by the edge of the river. Max himself was bent over, nursing his hand and swearing under his breath. Olivia stood panting, her sword in her hand, looking triumphant and just a little bit concerned.

"Umm, are you all right, Max?" she said.

"No, I'm not all right! I think you sliced my hand off, you maniac!" said Max through gritted teeth. "Honestly, Olivia — you are a total menace with a sword."

They had spent the afternoon lazing by the river, just a few miles from the castle, at a place where the woodland opened out around an old charcoal-burner's stone hut. There was a deep sandy pool there that was perfect for swimming. The shadows were just starting to get longer and it was nearly time to head back, when Olivia had challenged Max to a sword fight. He hadn't fenced with her for a few months, and he was taken aback by just how much better she'd become. Her manoeuvre might have been a bit unorthodox, but she'd disarmed him very effectively, and Max was smarting less from the injury than from the shame of being beaten by his younger sister.

Which meant that he was in no mood to deal with the mocking laughter that was now coming from the trees just a few yards away.

"So, Pendragon. You really *are* a bit of a loser, aren't you? Disarmed by your baby sister!"

The tall, thin figure of Snotty Hogsbottom emerged from behind the stone hut, followed as usual by Jerome Stodmarsh. Before Max could react, Snotty had bent down and picked up his sword from where it was lying. He balanced it in his hand, then looked over to the deep water in the middle of the pool.

"Give it back!" said Max hotly. "That's my sword!"

Snotty raised his eyebrows.

"Well, you're not taking very good care of it, are you? Leaving it lying around where anyone could pick it up. But don't worry, I'll give it back. *When* I feel like it."

Max took a step toward Snotty, but Jerome moved forward, looking particularly large, and Max hesitated.

Snotty laughed, and leaned back against a tree, waving the sword idly around in front of him.

"So, how are the magic lessons going? Learned to tell the difference between a cauldron and a kettle yet?"

Max ground his teeth. He was utterly fed up with Snotty's taunts, particularly coming on top of being humiliated by Olivia. He was not going to let Snotty lord it over him about magic.

"Actually, I don't really bother with cauldrons *or* kettles any more. That's for babies," he said, loftily. "I've been doing magic without potions."

Snotty narrowed his eyes. "Really?" he said. "I'd like to see you try."

Olivia looked anxiously from one to the other. She could tell Max was furious, and Snotty was sounding dangerously calm. Jerome was considerably bigger than either her or Max, if it came to a fight, and Adolphus, as usual, was never there when you needed him. He'd gone upriver a while ago looking for fish to catch, and there was no telling when he'd decide to come back.

"I tell you what," drawled Snotty, looking down his long nose at Max. "You do some magic 'without potions' and I'll give your sword back. How's that?"

Max nodded grimly. Olivia drew in her breath. Max had told her about turning himself into a dragonfly without any kind of potion, but it didn't sound to her like he'd been entirely in control of the process, and goodness knows what Snotty would get him to do. She was pretty sure Merlin would not be happy about him trying this kind of magic on his own, so far from the castle.

Snotty smiled lazily, and held out a large piece of grey flint he'd been concealing in his hand.

"All right then," he said. "Do an icespell on this bit of rock." And he tossed it over to Max.

Max caught the stone and looked at it carefully. There was something familiar about the colour, and the jagged edges reminded him of . . . what? He couldn't think.

He turned it over in his hands, getting the feel of it. An icespell would encase the stone in a solid lump of ice. It was quite a straightforward spell — if you had brewed it up in a cauldron and then dried it to a purplish powder. All you would have to do is sprinkle a few grains of the powder on the rock and say the right words. Max thought about the ingredients — bats' wingbeats, the itch of rosehip powder, slugs' eyeball slime — and the essence of each of them as they mixed together in the spell.

Olivia held her breath. Snotty looked on with an odd expression. Jerome cleaned his fingernails with his hunting knife.

Max made a decision. He held the stone in front of him and felt for the magic he knew was there, inside him, the magic he'd called on to make himself into a dragonfly. He willed it to make the shape of the icespell, and he directed it at the rock.

Nothing happened.

Max pressed his lips together and tried again, harder.

Still nothing happened.

Jerome started to snigger. Snotty was concentrating on the stone with a frown. Olivia bit her lip.

Max was puzzled. He'd felt the magic flow. He'd definitely felt it hit the stone and it should have been a solid lump of ice by now. But something was resisting the spell. It was as if the stone was enchanted, or bigger than it looked, or shielded somehow from his magic. It was some trick of Snotty's, he was sure of it. Well, Snotty was going to get a shock.

Max reached for every last drop of magic he

could gather and shaped it into the icespell. Just as he did so, he noticed a tiny ant crawling on the grey flint surface, and as quickly as he could, wove an extra thread into the spell to protect any living creature on the rock as it was iced. Then he flung the magic at the flint in a great flood of power.

The stone disappeared into the middle of a perfect sparkling crystal of solid ice.

Olivia let out her breath, and Max looked up in triumph at Snotty.

Snotty looked distinctly pale and slightly taken aback, but he recovered swiftly. He clapped slowly and turned to Jerome.

"Well, then, I suppose we'd better give him his sword back. He'll be needing it soon anyway, eh Jerome?"

Jerome, looking ever so slightly sick, nodded.

Max suddenly felt a slight twinge of doubt. What had he done? Had they tricked him? Why was Snotty looking so triumphant, and Jerome so sick?

Snotty threw Max's sword over, and it landed at

his feet with a clatter. Snotty laughed nastily.

"You know you've done something, Pendragon, don't you? You just don't know what! Well, we'll leave it to you to find out, shall we?"

And he turned his back and slipped away through the trees, Jerome following, crashing through the undergrowth like a small herd of boar. Silence fell on the clearing as Max and Olivia looked at each other.

What had he done?

Disaster at Camelot

It was Ferocious who broke the silence. He had watched the encounter between Max and Snotty with one eye open, while curled up for an afternoon doze on Max's pack. But now he jumped down and stretched.

"Well, it's no use looking like a wet fish, Max. Whatever you've done, you've done. Better just go and find out what it is."

At that moment there was a flurry of splashing and squawking as Adolphus crash-landed in the pool alongside a small duck, and both of them flapped their way noisily to the bank.

"Hello! Hello! I've made a friend! Come and meet him!" called Adolphus happily.

The duck waddled out of the water, with Adolphus bounding around him in circles, and bobbed his head at them all with a wide grin.

"Quack!" he said cheerily. "Got any bread?"

"What?" said Max, startled.

"*Got any bread?*" said the duck. "Only, I always ask. If it's humans. 'Cause they often do have. And I like a bit of bread."

"Umm, yes, I think so," said Max, and looked in his pack. There was an old dried-up piece of bread he'd stuffed in there at breakfast a few days ago, intending to eat it later. He broke it up and threw it into the water, where the duck happily splashed around finding every last bit.

"Quack!" he said, when it had all gone. "Much

obliged. Tasty bit of bread that. Got any more?"

"No, sorry," said Max.

"Ah, well, never mind. Maybe another time." And the duck dived under the surface for a second, splashed water over himself happily, then waddled out of the river.

"Pleased to meet you," he said, putting his head on one side and looking at Max and Olivia with one beady black eye. "So — what are we doing now?"

"We're going back to the castle," said Ferocious. "To see what wonders Max has managed to achieve with his latest spell. Probably turned all the fish in the moat to tadpoles or something."

"Oh, magic, eh?" said the duck. "Like a bit of magic myself. Got a lot of friends who do magic. Are you any good?" He looked at Max brightly, and Max coloured.

"Well," he said. "I'm not too bad. But things do have a habit of going wrong..."

He bit his lip, and hoped Ferocious was right and he'd only done something minor with the spell.

He had an awful feeling it was going to turn out to be much, much worse.

***

The sun was low as they reached the edge of the woodland. The duck, whose name was Vortigern, had decided to come with them to visit a distant cousin of his who lived in the castle duckpond. He had regaled them all the way with tales of his family and various adventures — it seemed that he was named after an ancient king, who had been saved from ambush by Vortigern's great-great-great grandfather. The king had gratefully made the whole family official Royal Ducks.

"So really, you ought to call me *King* Vortigern," he explained. "Or Your Highness. But I let my friends off."

Max had gradually relaxed as they trudged back, and was looking forward to a good dinner and Lancelot's new song. But as they rounded the corner and the castle came into full view, all thoughts of food disappeared. Max stood rooted to the spot, feeling like a vast weight had just dropped on top of him.

There, in the distance, should have been Camelot. But in its place, reaching up higher than even the tallest turret of the castle, was a mountain of ice, sparkling blue-white and sheer, right to the edges of the moat.

"Druid's toenails," breathed Olivia, awed. "What have you *done*, Max?"

They all looked at him, wide-eyed.

"Quack!" said Vortigern. "That's a corker! Did you do that all by yourself? My cousin's not going to be happy."

"Neither is anyone else," said Ferocious. "You've really done it this time, Max. Better take it off, quick."

Max sat down on the ground. He didn't think his legs would hold him up any more. He felt like he might be sick.

"You *can* take it off, Max?" said Olivia, looking anxiously at his pale face.

Max pulled the stone from his pocket and looked at it. It was still solid and covered in ice. None of it had melted.

"The thing is," he said in a small voice, "I didn't direct the spell at Camelot. I did it on the stone. There's some magic that's linked the stone to the castle, and I'm not sure I *can* reverse it. And there's something odd about the spell, too, because the ice should have melted by now and it hasn't." He looked at them miserably. "I tried taking the spell off the stone back at the clearing, after Snotty had gone. But I couldn't. And I'm pretty certain that means I can't take it off the castle either."

They looked at him, appalled. The castle was encased in a mountain of ice, which meant that everyone inside it was also encased in ice — King Arthur, Merlin, Sir Bertram ... And Max couldn't take the spell off.

"Wonderful," said Ferocious, who recovered first. "Excellent. Castle and all its inhabitants iced for an unknown amount of time, while we figure out how to break the spell. It's just as well we were all *outside* the castle when you did it, Max, or we'd *really* have been in a sticky situation."

Olivia gave a shaky laugh. "He's right, Max. It could have been worse. At least we're all here together. We'll find a way to reverse it . . . But I suppose . . . the people in the castle . . . they will be all right, won't they? When the spell comes off, I mean?" She was trying not to make too much of the question, but Max could see that she had gone rather white. He nodded.

"I'm pretty sure they will be. Luckily there was an ant on the stone, so I made sure there was a bit of the spell that protected anything alive on it while it was iced. *That* should mean the same thing applied to the castle."

"Well then," said Ferocious. "Nothing to worry about. Between us, we'll find a way to take the spell off, you'll see."

"Yes, yes!" said Adolphus, nodding vigorously. "And Vortigern will help, won't you?"

"Quack!" said Vortigern. "You can count on me. Always happy to help!"

Max nodded and felt a bit better. He looked again at the distant castle. He could see dark figures moving around by the gatehouse, which was just outside the moat and so the only part of the castle not encased in ice.

"Umm, Olivia," he said slowly. "Do you happen to remember who was on guard duty when we left?"

She considered. "Well . . . everyone important was in the meeting with King Arthur — the one about the mysterious sorceress. I think the only one on guard duty was . . . oh . . ." Her face fell. "It was Sir Richard."

"That's what I thought," said Max grimly. "Sir Richard Hogsbottom. Because he knew what was going to happen!"

Ferocious sniffed. "Well, in that case it's probably best if we don't just walk up to the castle and ask if they need any help. Or we'll be helping from the bottom of a very deep dungeon."

"Too right," said Olivia. "Maybe we'd better just go back to the woods."

Max thought about it. "I agree. We can head for the old charcoal-burner's hut. But first I think we need to know what they're planning. Which means getting a bit closer, without being seen."

"Oh, yes," said Adolphus eagerly. "I can do that! I'm very good at creeping. Look — look at me doing invisible creeping!"

He wriggled along the ground on his belly, squawking slightly as he scraped over stones, and not quite in control of his tail, which waved enthusiastically every few yards.

"Yes, Adolphus, very good," said Olivia encouragingly. "But you're a bit big. I think it might be better to send Ferocious."

"Yes, me as usual, into the mouth of danger. Ha! Never fear, Ferocious is always ready to risk life and limb," said the rat, and sighed.

"Quack! I'll go, too! Might get some bread from the guards!" said Vortigern.

"Right," said Max. "Good idea. Vortigern, you can act as a decoy — distract the guards while Ferocious gets closer and tries to find out what Sir Richard's up to."

***

Ferocious crept quietly along the floor of the gatehouse, under the wooden benches by the side of the wall. Vortigern was already outside, quacking loudly, and most of the guards were competing to see who could get a piece of bread straight into his open beak from ten yards. Inside, one of the gate guards was discussing the situation with Sir Lionel, who had just arrived from Leogrance.

"It's been a complete nightmare! We've tried chipping our way into the castle but the ice is like solid rock! Nothing can seem to break it."

Sir Lionel stroked his moustache. "It's obviously an enchantment, and I never was any use when it came to magic. It's a good thing Sir Richard was outside the castle when it happened — at least he knows a bit more about these things!"

Ferocious sniffed. Sir Richard Hogsbottom, Snotty's father, knew hardly anything about magic — but he knew a great deal about plotting. He was almost certainly in on the whole thing, and was bound to have something nasty up his wide velvet sleeve.

"Yes, well, he's outside having a look at the ice now, with young Adrian," said the guard. "And he's sent a swift to Lady Morgana le Fay — she may be able to help, of course. Hopefully the answer will be back soon."

Almost as he spoke, the great door of the gatehouse crashed open and Snotty walked in, with his father behind him. Sir Richard was a short, rather tubby knight, with an ingratiating manner. He smiled around at them all, looking very pleased with himself, and then seemed to remember that the occasion was a solemn one and changed his expression to one of concern.

"I fear there's nothing I can do. Even Adrian, who is *very* skilled in magic, cannot make a dent in it."

"I'm afraid so," nodded Snotty. "It's quite likely that they're all dead." His eyes gleamed, and his mouth gave the tiniest twitch of triumph as he said it.

"Er, well — we can't be sure of that," said Sir Richard quickly. "It's entirely possible they are simply frozen temporarily . . . We will have to wait and see."

As he spoke, a small white bird darted into the room and hovered in front of them. Sir Richard plucked it out of the air, and it immediately transformed into a small folded piece of parchment.

"Ah, the return swift from my lady Morgana," he said with satisfaction, and opened it. He looked around. "She says she will come at once. She may be able to remove the spell without anyone being hurt — at least, she will do her best. And in the meantime, she will accept the position of queen — temporarily, of course — in Arthur's place. She will be here in three days."

"Well, that's a relief," said Sir Lionel heartily. "If anyone can sort this blasted sorceress out, it's Lady

Morgana. So — we'll just do our best to guard the castle, keep the peace and wait for her to arrive, eh?"

Ferocious had heard enough. He sneaked carefully out of the gatehouse and hurried back to the others. When they heard what Ferocious had to report, Max looked grim, and so did Olivia.

Lady Morgana was due in three days, so they had to find a way to take the spell off before she got here. Because if Morgana was the one who removed the spell, there was absolutely no chance that either Arthur or Merlin would survive the disenchantment process.

Adolphus Has a Plan

Vortigern the duck had found a nice sheltered corner of the wall just outside the gatehouse door. The moon was beginning to rise over the black outline of the hills to the east of the castle, and the icy mountain behind him was shimmering with a pale white translucence. The few soldiers still guarding the boundaries of what used to be Castle Camelot were moving quietly, their armour clinking slightly as they shifted position, peering into the darkness.

Vortigern was considering what to do. He had heard quite a bit about Morgana le Fay from his cousin Guido. Guido regularly found his pond disturbed by the arrival of rather startled castle servants, transported fully clothed and upside down into the mud whenever they annoyed the visiting sorceress. Vortigern was rather curious to see the lady herself. And the soldiers in the gatehouse had bread, and were willing to share it. But on the other hand, Max was clearly quite a magical person, too. And Adolphus was a lot of fun. And he rather thought there was still a bit of bread left in Max's pack. The duck stretched, ruffled his feathers and waddled quietly toward the river.

***

It was an hour before Max and Olivia stumbled wearily back to the stretch of river where they'd spent the afternoon. Even Adolphus had lost some of his bounce. The trees around the clearing were shades of silver or grey, while the old stones of the charcoal-burner's hut shone pale white in the moonlight, its shadow stretching out into the woods like an inky pool.

Inside, the hut was dusty and full of cobwebs hanging from every beam and corner, but when Olivia investigated the cupboards she found jars of preserves, nuts, dried fruit, blankets and firewood. Soon they had a warm fire crackling in the hearth, a bowl of nuts and sweet, wrinkled, old apples balanced between them and a couple of musty blankets to lie on. If it hadn't been for the dead weight in his stomach every time he remembered Camelot buried under a ton of ice, Max might actually have enjoyed the sense of adventure.

"So," said Olivia, as she bit into one of the apples and threw another to Max. "What do you think?"

Max grimaced. "I've been trying to work it out. I'm pretty sure it's something to do with that spell Snotty was planting the other day. The stone he gave me — it's exactly like the chip of stone that was in the middle of his spell powder. I *knew* I recognized it but I couldn't think of where I'd seen it before."

"Do you think that's what made the connection between your spell and Camelot?" asked Olivia.

Ferocious emerged from Max's belt pouch and scampered over to the bowl to get himself a nut.

"Of course it's the connection, pea-brain," he observed, spitting out a bit of hard shell. "Snotty must have spread them all over the castle — didn't he say that that was 'the last one?'"

"Yes, he did," said Max. "And he also said it had to be against the northernmost wall. I wonder ... Maybe he had one in each direction — east, west, north, south. That would be enough to bring the whole castle into the spell. Rotten, back-stabbing slimeball!"

They sat for a moment, contemplating Snotty's complete and absolute treachery. Then Olivia frowned and threw her apple core in the fire.

"What I don't understand though, Max, is how you managed to ice the whole of Camelot. Even if the stone *was* somehow connected to the castle.

That's a bit of a massive spell, isn't it? You'd need an enormous amount of magic to do something like that, wouldn't you?"

Max bit his lip. He'd been hoping no one would think of that particular question. It was the aspect of the whole disaster he felt most guilty about. He *had* known there was something odd about the stone. He *had* known something big was preventing the icespell from working, and he should have stopped. But he didn't want to back down in front of Snotty. He was angry and determined to show off his new-found skill, and he had gone ahead and thrown every ounce of his magic at the jagged grey flint. And he had iced Camelot — the whole castle. It was all his fault.

He looked up and found Olivia watching him still, her eyebrows raised.

"Well, I . . . er . . . I did quite a massive spell," he admitted. "It didn't work with only a small one — and I thought maybe Snotty was blocking it somehow . . . But it must have been the fact that I was actually spelling the whole castle."

Ferocious whistled. "Well blow me down with a dragonfly's wing, Max. That's *some* magic you've got there. I thought maybe Morgana had done an increasing spell on the rock or something. But if you did it all yourself, why can't you take it off?"

Max sighed. "I think it's because of the connection spell. I'd have to take that off before I could reverse my own spell, and Morgana's magic is really tricky — not just strong, but almost impossible for anyone else to undo. The only person I know who can unravel her spells is Merlin, and he's inside the castle."

There was a silence as they thought about the fact that everyone they would normally rely on for help — Merlin, King Arthur, Sir Bertram, even Lancelot — were all stuck inside the ice mountain. Suddenly Adolphus lifted his head.

"Er — can anyone hear anything?" he said.

They listened. There was a slight rustling in the undergrowth outside the hut. They held their breath, keeping as still as possible. The rustling seemed to be getting nearer, and then it stopped. They sat in silence, staring wide-eyed at each other, waiting to see if there was any more movement. Then, erupting into the stillness with an enormous CRASH, something hurtled through the single window of the hut right into the middle of the floor.

"Aaarrghh! Help! Save me!" shrieked Adolphus as they all scrambled rapidly away from the dark shadowy creature that was flapping noisily around in front of them.

"Quack!" it said loudly. "Got any bread?"

"Vortigern!" exclaimed Olivia. "What on earth? You gave us a real shock! What are you doing here?"

"Followed you," said the duck happily. "I was going to stick around to see Lady Morgana do her stuff — I like a bit of magic myself — but then I thought, well, Max is quite a magical sort, and Adolphus is my new chum, and you have bread. You *do* have bread, don't you?" he added anxiously.

"I do, as it happens," said Max, laughing. After

all the tension, the sudden arrival of the duck had left him feeling rather hysterical. He dug out his pack, and broke off a small piece of one of the rolls left from their picnic. Vortigern gobbled it up, and then bobbed his head in thanks.

"Right then," he said. "What's the plan? I mean, seeing as I'm the nearest thing you have to royalty, I'm assuming I'm the leader. So I'd better know the plan."

Max caught Olivia's eye and they both grinned. Vortigern was probably the least royal-looking creature you could imagine. But he had a certain bumptious confidence, and he'd made them all feel a lot more cheerful. They could certainly do much worse for a leader.

"We've got to find a way to take the spell off Camelot," said Max. "I can't do it — I can't undo Morgana's magic. And I don't know anyone who can, except Merlin."

"Who's currently deep in the middle of a mountain of ice," put in Ferocious.

"And we don't have any horses, or supplies, and Morgana's three days away from taking over the kingdom," said Olivia.

"Quack ... Tricky," Vortigern said, then looked over at Adolphus. "Adolphus? You got any ideas for a plan?"

Ferocious snorted, and Max and Olivia tried not to smile. Only someone who didn't know Adolphus would turn to him for ideas. They all loved him dearly, but there was no doubt that the small dragon was hopelessly dim.

Adolphus bounced up and down happily. A plan! He'd been asked to come up with a plan! He closed one eye, stuck out his tongue, waved his tail and concentrated very, very hard. Camelot was covered in ice ... They needed to get rid of the ice ... Umm ... He breathed a bit of fire to clear his head and then suddenly he had it! An idea! Ice was very cold, and fire was very hot. They just needed lots and lots of fire. They needed ...

"Great-Aunt Wilhelmina!" he triumphantly

shouted. "Why don't we ask Great-Aunt Wilhelmina? She can breath fire at it!"

Ferocious rolled his eyes. "Adolphus, you twit, this is a *magic* mountain of ice, not a build-up of frost on a cold night. You can't melt an icespell..."

But Max had jumped up in delight. "You've got it, Adolphus! Well done, you're a genius!" he cried. "Great-Aunt Wilhelmina! Of course!"

"Um, sorry?" said Ferocious, taken aback. "You do know fire won't work, don't you, Max?"

"Yes, yes, I know," said Max happily. "It's not that. It's that Great-Aunt Wilhelmina is a dragon. A very ancient dragon. And dragons are magical creatures. A dragon as old as Great-Aunt Wilhelmina is *bound* to know a way to reverse the icespell."

"Brilliant!" said Olivia. "Well done, Adolphus!"

"Yes, yes," said Adolphus, excitedly. "Well done me, whoopee! We're going to see Great-Aunt Wilhelmina again! She'll melt the icespell! Hurrah!" He flapped his wings and grinned, bouncing joyfully around the hut until he tripped over the basket of wood and crashed into the wall with a thud.

"Umm — ouch," he said, and sat down looking slightly cross-eyed.

"Right then," said Vortigern. "That's the plan. Great-Aunt Wilhelmina, first thing tomorrow. But right now, we all need to get some rest. So off to bed everyone. Quack, quack!"

He waddled around, herding them all toward the fire and the spread-out blankets with loud quacks and flapping wings. When they were all settled down, he bobbed his head in approval, then tucked it under his wing and went to sleep.

Olivia opened one eye and grinned at Max.

"Well, we've got a leader, and we've got a plan. Things are looking up."

Max nodded. He felt a lot better now they had someone to go to for help. Dragons were hugely magical, although they didn't start to develop their magic till they were about a hundred, so Adolphus had a long way to go. But Great-Aunt Wilhelmina was four hundred and forty-three. He remembered the last time they'd met her, up in Gore, and the power he'd felt in her piercing golden eyes. If anyone could help them sort out the icespell, it was Great-Aunt Wilhelmina.

An Encounter with Snotty Hogsbottom

Olivia woke up early in the morning, cold and stiff. Pale light was filtering through the single window, and every tree outside seemed to have its own orchestra of birds, each competing with the others to be the noisiest. She groaned, and turned to pull the blankets over her head and go back to sleep, but the others were also stirring and soon Vortigern was chivvying them all into getting up.

"Come along, come along, haven't got all day. Bread first, then we need to set off. Quack, quack!" And he waddled outside for a quick splash in the river.

Olivia opened one eye and looked at Max, who was blearily rubbing his face.

"Does Vortigern *have* to be leader?" she whispered.

Max made a face.

"I'm not sure we've got any choice. But anyway, he's right. We have to get going."

"Yes, but where to?" asked Ferocious, emerging yawning from a wrinkle of blankets in the corner. "In all the planning last night, I think I must have missed the bit where we actually found out where Great-Aunt Wilhelmina *is*. For all we know, she's gone back to Gore."

"Umm ... good point," said Max, and felt his heart sink. "Adolphus?" he called. "Do you actually know where your great aunt is?"

Adolphus nodded his head happily and grinned.

"Well, she said ... she was going to ... I know

she told me, but, er, well . . . no. Not exactly. Sorry!"

"Wonderful," said Ferocious. "Now what?"

At that moment Vortigern waddled back into the hut. He stopped when he saw their downcast faces.

"Quack!" he said. "Cheer up! Time for bread!"

"Vortigern," said Ferocious. "I don't care if you are first in line to the throne of the Roman Empire, if you mention bread one more time I will personally bite your beak off." And he displayed his sharp white teeth.

Vortigern bobbed his head and quacked.

"Not to worry. It's just, I do like a bit of . . . Well, anyway. Why all the long faces?"

"We don't know where Great-Aunt Wilhelmina is," said Max. "So we can't go and ask her for a reversal spell."

"Oh, is that all?" said the duck cheerily. "Well that's okay, then. Because I know exactly where she is."

"You do?" said Olivia, surprised. "How come *you* know Great-Aunt Wilhelmina?"

"Well, I did say I like a bit of magic. Always

make it a point to introduce myself to any new magic users in the area. And Lady Wilhelmina came down here, oh, must have been a month ago now. As a matter of fact, I showed her the cave she's staying in now. Down by the sea."

"Yes, yes," said Adolphus happily. "That's it! By the sea. I *knew* that's what she said. Yippee! I remembered!"

"The thing is," said the duck, thoughtfully, "it's a bit of a way. Down in the west. Takes me about half a day to fly it ... but walking, it could be a couple of days or more. Not sure we can do it on foot and be back before Lady Morgana gets here."

"Could we get some horses from the castle?" suggested Olivia. "Or — Max! Could you change us into something? Maybe we could be dragons, then we could *all* fly!"

"Er — no thanks," said Ferocious swiftly. "Me and Adolphus will go together, won't we Adolphus? We're old hands at flying together, eh? Not that I don't trust you, Max, your new magic without potions is very impressive, but, well, I think I'd rather stay as a rat, this time ..."

Max grinned. "It's all right, Ferocious, I won't change you into an earwig by mistake. I'm pretty sure I can manage this one, I did it with Merlin."

"All the same, very kind of you Max, but I'm fine as a rat," said Ferocious, scampering over to Adolphus and climbing up onto his back.

Max looked at Olivia. "I can change us into something, but we might have to rely on Great-Aunt Wilhelmina to turn us back."

She took a deep breath.

"We've got to get there as quickly as we can, Max. I trust you. Do what you have to."

Max thought about the long trip west, and decided that it would make more sense to be a bird — much less noticeable than a dragon. Last time he and Olivia had been dragons, they'd nearly been caught in the Castle Gore dragon hunt. He thought about the bird he knew best, the hunting kestrel he and Olivia shared back at Castle Perilous. He thought about the bird's bright black eyes, her questioning look, her curved beak and mottled reddish-brown feathers and the power in her strong wings. Then he felt for the magic inside him, gathered it up and threw it at himself and Olivia.

BANG!

Suddenly everything seemed brighter, and sharper. He realized that his vision was about a thousand times better, and he could hear the whisper of a small insect scurrying across the wooden floor. At the same time he could feel the power and strength in his shoulder muscles as they flexed his great wings. He looked across at Olivia, and gulped.

She was, like him, a kestrel, and he could tell that she was equally awed at the effects of the transformation. But she was bright pink.

He looked down at himself, and had to laugh. He was also bright pink, with mottled bits of purple.

"Never mind, Max," said Olivia. "It's amazing! *Much* better than being a frog! I feel like I could fly for hours. Race you!"

She swooped out of the hut and rose into the air with short, powerful wingbeats, circling to gain height. Even from a hundred feet up, she could see every tiny detail of the clearing beneath them, every movement of the leaves in the wind, every ripple in the water as a fish rose to take a fly. The sun was coming up, and the day was going to be a sunny one. Simply for the joy of it, Olivia put her beak down and dived, hurtling toward the ground at an incredible speed, then pulling up just inches from the surface of the river and gliding gently to a branch overhanging the stone hut.

"Quack!" said Vortigern, and flew up to the branch to join her. "Very impressive. I do like to see magic done, gives me a tingling feeling all through my feathers. Right then, you lot. Are we ready to go?"

***

Max glided along, riding the air currents high above the river, his wings carefully dipping and twisting to keep him level. He looked down, following the progress of a couple of riders gently ambling along the road west from Camelot. Suddenly he stiffened, and focused on them more closely. There was something about the rider in front ... Just then, the rider lifted his head, and looked straight up at Max, his pale face and spiky black hair perfectly visible. It was Snotty Hogsbottom.

Max hesitated for a second, and then dived. He was so angry he barely thought about what he would do when he got down there, but it had something to do with claws, beaks and wings, and the desired result definitely involved Snotty falling off his horse.

But the riders had seen him coming and pulled up under a nearby tree. Snotty had his sword out and he was waving it dangerously around his head. Max hovered for a second, then settled on a branch just above the waving sword.

"Back off, Pendragon!" shouted Snotty. "I know it's you, because I've got a direction spell set on you and I've been following you all morning. And don't think you can get away from me — however fast you fly, you've still got to wait for that potty duck you're with, and we're not going to be far behind you. So don't think you're going to be doing any heroic rescuing this time."

"Er — Adrian?" Jerome said hesitantly, plucking at Snotty's sleeve. "Are you sure that's Max? You're not just ranting at some strange bird, are you?"

"Don't be such a turnip head, Jerome," said Snotty dismissively. "I'd recognize that loser anywhere, even if he has turned himself into a bird. Besides, only Pendragon could have turned himself into a *pink* kestrel."

Max ground his teeth at his inability to communicate just what he thought of Snotty, but before he could even screech, Snotty looked up and shook his head.

"You know, I never thought you'd actually do it. Lady Morgana has been keeping a close eye on your progress with Merlin, and she said you would — you'd take the bait *and* you'd do the spell. Turns out she was right, as usual. And she's only two days away from being queen now, so you'd better watch out. If you show any signs of finding out how to reverse the spell before she gets here, I've been given the job of sorting you out ... And it will be my pleasure." He smiled, and his eyes gleamed with malice. "In fact, maybe I'll just do it anyway, before you get a chance. What do you think, Jerome? Roast kestrel for supper?"

He reached behind for his bow, and had an arrow on the string before Max could blink. Max took off just as he loosed it, and the arrow whistled past his tail feathers as he soared rapidly into the sky, seething with rage.

Snotty Hogsbottom! One of these days he was going to find a way to get even with that slimy, no-good, poisonous slug's backside. But in the meantime, he was *not* going to let Snotty find out where they were going. Drawing on every bit of magic he could mentally lay his hands on, while also trying to control his wings, Max flung a misdirection spell out behind him. With any luck, it would at least slow Snotty down while they got a chance to consult Great-Aunt Wilhelmina.

The Dragon's Cave

It turned out that Vortigern had been a little over-optimistic about the time it would take to get to Great-Aunt Wilhelmina's cave. Even if they'd flown non-stop it would have been afternoon by the time they got there. As it was, with frequent stops for a rest and a paddle, and a lot of catching fish, the sun was low over the horizon when they finally crested the last hill and saw land give way to endless blue sea.

Max blinked, dazzled for a moment by the brightness of the sun reflecting off the water, and glided down to a stunted old tree by the shore. The sea was startlingly blue, with constantly shifting, peeling waves smashing down in spumes of spray, one after the other, as they rolled into the shore. The water swirled around jagged rocks and ran up the pebbly beach before being sucked back with a rattling roar into the oncoming waves.

Max had seen the sea once or twice before, but not for a few years. He rested, gripping the branch he was perched on tightly, as gusts of wind buffeted him and blew his feathers all the wrong way, tasting the salt in the air and watching the gulls wheeling overhead. They were dancing in and out of each other's way, occasionally getting caught by the spray from a particularly huge wave and calling out in their harsh voices.

"Isn't it brilliant?" gasped Olivia, as she landed beside him. "I'd forgotten how big the sea is. And how wild!"

"Quack!" said Vortigern, landing just by the tree in a not very elegant flurry of wings. "Bit windy!"

Next moment, Adolphus too had dropped out of the sky next to them, and a very ruffled-looking Ferocious crawled thankfully off his back, trying to smooth his fur back to its normal sleekness.

"Tail and whiskers! We're here at last. I almost think I might let you turn me into a bird for the trip back, Max. I'd forgotten that Adolphus flies like a maniac crossed with a bouncing ball. Nearly fell off a hundred miles back and haven't dared move ever since..."

"Umm, Max," said Olivia, with one eye on the seagulls wheeling close by. "I think we'd better be human again, if you can manage it. Those birds aren't looking very friendly."

Max looked up. She was right. The gulls were not pleased to be sharing their beach with two strangely coloured birds of prey, and looked like they might get nasty at any minute. Max closed his eyes and thought hard about being human again.

Crack!

The branch they were sitting on snapped under their combined weight, and the two of them, fully human, were deposited on the ground with a thud.

"Ouch!" said Max, rubbing his shoulder. "I didn't think it would work, or I'd have got down from the branch before I changed back."

"Well, great magic, Max, but next time warn me," said Olivia feelingly, as she tried to stand up. "I think I might have broken several small bones and bruised the rest of them."

"Enough complaining," said Ferocious unsympathetically. "We're on a mission. We need to find a dragon. Lead on, Your Royal Duckness!"

***

Great-Aunt Wilhelmina's cave stretched far back into the cliff, so far that you could hardly hear the distant boom and crash of the sea. A small, narrow split between two immense rock faces widened into a passageway, and that in turn opened out into an immense cavern. It should have been quite dark, but it shone with a greenish white glow that came from the same eerie spheres of light Max remembered from the last time he'd met the dragon, deep in a mountain in the misty lakeland of Gore.

Great-Aunt Wilhelmina lay stretched out on the flat sandy floor of the cave, her huge head turned toward them, her amber eyes watching them approach.

"Well, well. If it isn't my dear nephew, A-drip-nose, and his companions . . . And Your Royal Highness. What a pleasure," she rumbled, in her deep voice.

"Greetings, Lady Wilhelmina," quacked Vortigern. "Got any — well — er . . ."

"I do indeed have bread," said the dragon with a wide grin, and she pushed a small, low table toward them, which was piled with bread, meat, fruit, pastries and flagons of hot, spiced apple juice. "I had a feeling I might be having some guests . . ."

Adolphus bounded forward joyfully and got into a large platter of roasted caterpillars. The rest of the feast looked delicious, and Max suddenly realized how fantastically hungry he was. He bowed to the great dragon, and thanked her for her hospitality.

"Think nothing of it, young Pendragon," she boomed. "Always glad to see another magic user . . . How did you get on with that cauldron I gave you?"

In between mouthfuls of pastry and swigs of apple juice, Max and Olivia told her the story of their adventures in Gore, how Olivia had been sent to the Otherworld by Morgana, and how they'd been able to use the cauldron to rescue her and bring King Arthur and his companions back safely. Vortigern, who had not heard the story before, got quite excited, and kept interrupting. When they described Olivia's masterful cauldron throw, which had knocked out the Silent Sentinel and saved Arthur's life, he whooped and turned three somersaults.

But all too soon, the feast was finished and the story over. Great-Aunt Wilhelmina turned her golden eyes on Max and looked at him with a quizzical expression.

"So, young Pendragon, what brings you here? I had a feeling in my bones I would see you again, but I didn't think it would be quite so soon."

Max swallowed hard. He wasn't sure where to begin. As he hesitated, Adolphus bounced over and thumped the floor of the cave enthusiastically with his tail.

"We need you to breathe fire. It was all my idea. Vortigern asked for a plan — and I came up with one! Me! We need someone to breathe lots and lots of fire and melt the ice." He looked up at Great-Aunt Wilhelmina expectantly, and breathed a little fire of his own, as if to show her just what he meant.

"Ice?" she rumbled. "You need me to melt some *ice*? Is that *all*?" She sounded extremely offended at the idea that she was wanted simply as a very large mobile bonfire.

"No, no, that's not it at all," said Max hurriedly. "Adolphus has got it a bit mixed up. We have an ice problem, but it's not fire we need. It's a spell."

Great-Aunt Wilhelmina narrowed her eyes. "So. An icespell. Which you can't undo yourself? Where is it, and who cast it, may I ask?"

Max coloured. "It was me. And it's on Camelot."

"Camelot?" she said, looking surprised. "The whole castle?"

"Yes," said Max, in a small voice. "I got tricked into it. And the spell that tricked me was made by Morgana, so I can't seem to undo it."

Max waited for the old dragon to tell him what a foolish boy he'd been, and how wizards should never ever be tempted to show off. But to his surprise she did neither of these things. She widened her eyes, took a deep breath and hooted with laughter.

"Iced the *whole* castle? The whole castle? My dear boy, what a spectacular idiot you are! Morgana must be rubbing her hands in glee!"

She snorted in delight, breathing little gusts of blue-white flame from her nostrils and waving her long green tail as she laughed. Finally she stopped. She wiped her eyes with a great claw and grinned at Max.

"Haven't laughed so much in years. Not since Merlin ... Well, anyway. Knew you'd be good value, Max, back when I gave you my special cauldron. So. We'll have to do something about this and stop that dreadful sorceress, won't we?"

"So you *can* reverse the spell," said Max, thankfully. "We were hoping you could."

"Oh, no, not me," said Great-Aunt Wilhelmina, shaking her head. "We'll have to ask the Lady. She's a bit potty, but she's very powerful and she's got a soft spot for Merlin. I'm sure she'll find a way to sort it all out. But not till morning. Can't get to the Lady till sunrise. So we may as well get some rest. Come along, A-dormouse and Your Royal Highness, there's a nice waterfall back here to shower in, and comfortable beds all around."

Max exchanged glances with Olivia, and she gave him a thumbs-up. It looked like Great-Aunt

Wilhelmina was going to help, and it seemed like she had a good idea of what to do. They followed her to the back of the cave, where there was indeed a small waterfall, as well as a deep pool in which Vortigern was already happily splashing around, quacking loudly. Next to the pool was a pile of soft, richly embroidered blankets. Olivia fell onto the pile with a sigh, and closed her eyes.

"Fantastic. I feel like I could sleep for a week."

"Not quite so long, please, my dear," said Great-Aunt Wilhelmina with a rumbling laugh. "We need to be up well before dawn. I'll wake you when it's time. And in the meantime, A-dog's-nose, maybe you could come and sit with me and tell me all the family news . . ."

Adolphus danced alongside her to the front of the cave, chatting away. The greenish light faded as they went, leaving the area around the pool in a gentle dusky darkness.

Ferocious jumped onto Max's shoulder and gently nipped his ear.

"Time for sleep, Max. Been a long day. Lots of magic and too much fear of death by falling off Adolphus's back."

Max grinned, and tickled Ferocious behind the ears. Then he settled down on the pile of blankets with a yawn.

"Any idea who this Lady is we're going to see?" he asked sleepily, as Olivia started to snore.

"Nope," said Ferocious. "Must be some witch or other. Better hope she's a match for that evil old hag Morgana, eh, Max?"

But Max was already asleep, dreaming of ice and dragons and flying down an endless dark tunnel looking for something that wasn't there.

The Lady of the Island

The Lady, when they met her, was planting cabbages, and looked almost as unmagical as it is possible for a person to look. She was plump, with a kind brown face and long frizzy brown hair that was scattered with grey. As she reached up to brush her hair off her face, she left streaks of mud across her forehead and under her grey-blue eyes. There was something about her expression, however, that reminded Max very strongly of Merlin.

They had left the cave in darkness, with all of them piled on Great-Aunt Wilhelmina's back, even Adolphus.

"You wouldn't be able to get there on your own, A-doll's-house," she had rumbled. "Not magic enough yet."

As the sky had gradually lightened, they'd flown due south out to sea, and then, as the tip of the sun started to show over the eastern horizon, Great-Aunt Wilhelmina had gathered her strength and flown straight and fast into the light of the sunrise. One moment they were being dazzled by the dawn, the next moment a great island was rising up in front of them, and the huge dragon was coasting to an elegant landing next to a small vegetable patch. And there was the Lady, looking up to greet them. She showed no surprise at their sudden appearance.

"I'm afraid I am in the middle of the cabbages," apologized the Lady, smiling. "I did get some food and drink ready for you all when I realized you'd be

coming — but I can't remember where I left it ..."
She considered for a moment, then brightened. "Try
the woodshed, while I just get these planted in ..."

She waved a muddy hand vaguely at an old shed
further down the garden, and then went back to her
planting. Great-Aunt Wilhelmina motioned them to
follow, and they all headed after her with a
respectful nod at the back of the Lady, who was now
absorbed in tucking little plants into the soil.

The woodshed was full of logs, various garden
implements and rusty bits of what looked like an old
plough. But on an upturned wooden box in one corner
was a bowl of red apples and a jug of water. Max
realized he'd had no breakfast at exactly the same
time as Olivia, and they both dived for the bowl. The
apples tasted better than anything he'd ever eaten, and
the water was cold, clear and like drinking the most
perfect nectar. In among the apples, Max noticed,
were nuts for Ferocious, while small morsels that
looked suspiciously like roasted woodlice were
rapidly disappearing down Adolphus's throat.

"So glad you could drop by," said the Lady, entering the shed and settling herself on an old wheelbarrow while she wiped her hands clean on her skirt. When they were only very slightly less muddy, she pushed back her frizzy hair with both hands, wound it around into a loose knot behind her head, and tucked the ends down the back of her blouse.

"That's better," she said, smiling. "I can see you all properly now. Right — it's a spell you need, is it? Something big, I gather, that needs unravelling?"

Max took a deep breath and nodded.

"It's my fault. I did an icespell on a stone." He fished the grey flint, still encased in ice, out of his belt pouch, and showed it to the Lady. "It was magically connected to Camelot by Lady Morgana le Fay, and so I accidentally iced the whole castle. And Merlin's trapped in there, along with King Arthur, and, well . . . a lot of other people."

The Lady raised her eyebrows.

"Indeed. That's quite a spell, young man."

She took the stone from Max gingerly and held

it up to her right eye. She hummed a little, then threw the stone up in the air and caught it. Then she stuck her tongue out and tasted it.

"Uuurghh!" she said, and made a face. "Yes — definitely Morgana's magic. I'd know it anywhere. And poor dear Merlin is trapped inside?" She peered at the rock as if she expected to see the tiny figure of Merlin inside the ice, and then pursed her lips.

"Dear me. What a tangle. We'll have to see what we can do. It might take a while. In the meantime, I've got a job for you all!"

She stood up quickly and ushered them out of the shed, then she set off at a rapid stride around the back of a little stone house, toward what looked like a small orchard. As they followed the Lady, they saw that the stone wall around the orchard had been knocked down in one place and the stones were scattered around on the grass.

"The island's bull," she explained, gesturing to the wall. "He likes the apples, and he's forever destroying the wall to get to them. If you could just build it back up like sweet children, I'll go with Wilhelmina and prepare your spell."

And she hurried off, unknotting her hair as she went, so it flew out around her shoulders, then stooping to gather a few herbs on her way to the house.

"Well," said Max. "This seems simple enough. Just pile all the stones back into the wall."

"Hmm," said Ferocious thoughtfully. "I've got a feeling it might be a bit trickier than it seems."

Ferocious was right. They carefully gathered up the scattered stones and started slotting them back into the gap, with Adolphus doing a lot of the fetching and carrying, and Ferocious doing most of the directing from a perch on top of the nearest bit of unbroken wall. But after an hour of sweaty work the gap seemed no smaller, and the number of scattered stones in the grass looked exactly the same.

"Maybe we need to do it more quickly," suggested Olivia, so they redoubled their efforts. But after another half hour, Max thought he was going to expire, and Adolphus had given up and rolled over onto his back with his tongue out. The wall looked exactly as it had at the beginning.

"We need to think about this," said Ferocious. "There's obviously a trick to it."

"No trick!" came a voice from the trees on the other side of the wall. "Quite easy, really. Quack!"

"Vortigern!" said Max. "I wondered where you'd gone!"

"Went with the Lady," said the duck, emerging from the orchard. "She had some bread ... Anyway, I heard her talking to Lady Wilhelmina about the wall. It's a people wall. You have to say the name of a person your spell will help, and the stone stays put."

"Oh, well, why didn't we think of that before? How incredibly *obvious*," said Ferocious grumpily. "Right, then. Better get going before it's midnight. Come on, Max. A stone for Merlin."

Max heaved a large, flat stone into position and said, "Merlin." Then he stood and watched the stone carefully. It seemed to stay — but then again, he hadn't actually noticed any of the other stones disappearing, either. They just somehow didn't manage to amount to a wall, however many you put there.

Olivia dragged up another, placed it next to Max's and declared theatrically, "For King Arthur!" Again, it seemed like the stone was going to stay, but it was hard to tell.

"Come on," said Max. "We'll just have to carry on and see what happens in the end."

They dragged up more stones — for their father, for Lancelot, for Sir Patrick, for Sir Gareth, for Sir Boris... The wall was definitely getting higher, but not as quickly as it should have been. By the time they had run through every knight and lady in Camelot, it was half built, and they had to start on the squires.

"For Mordred," said Olivia through gritted teeth. "For Peredur... for Percival... for Roderick..."

After that, it was the castle servants, the soldiers, the cooks, the stable lads.

Finally, the wall was almost complete. There was only one stone left, but try as they might, no one could think of a single other person in the castle.

"The hawk boy," said Max. "Richard."

"No — done him," said Olivia.

"Oh — I know!" said Adolphus. "King Arthur!"

They all rolled their eyes.

"Sir Lionel?" said Ferocious.

"No — he was outside the castle, remember?" said Max.

There was a silence. The Max clicked his fingers.

"Fred!" he said triumphantly. "Fred the kitchen boy!"

They lifted the stone into place and together they all shouted, "Fred!"

The stone stayed. The wall was perfect.

As they stood back to admire it, Great-Aunt Wilhelmina appeared. The Lady was beside her, and when she saw the wall, she clapped her hands.

"Oh, thank you, my dears!" she cried. "That wall's been waiting years for a really good emergency! So nice to see it whole again. Come along up to the house and have some cake, and I'll show you the spell I've made."

A Spell and a Chase

It was dark inside Great-Aunt Wilhelmina's cave. Without the dragon, the globe lights dotted around the walls gave out only a faint glow, and the two figures creeping around kept bumping into each other, or tripping up.

"Ow, Jerome! Druid's toenails, keep your clodhopping feet off my toes!" hissed one of the figures.

"Sorry Adrian," said the other, sounding

utterly fed up. Jerome Stodmarsh had often wished he was not Sir Richard Hogsbottom's ward, but at that precise moment, creeping around the cave of an enormous and powerful dragon who might come back at any moment and decide to eat them, he really, *really* wished he wasn't. He even wished he'd taken his chances with Sir Garth the Grumpy, in his tiny hovel of a castle in the dull backwater of Avonmouth, instead. Then he wouldn't have been dragged on any of these dangerous and unpleasant missions with Adrian, who bossed him around like he was a servant. He could just have got on with the business of learning to be a knight, and spent his spare time with his collection of pet snails.

Jerome sighed, and tiptoed after the shadowy figure ahead.

"Here," hissed Snotty, as Jerome caught up with him. "There's a small gap in the rock. I think it's wide enough for both of us to hide inside ... and I'll sprinkle darkness powder just in front, should keep us fairly invisible. It must be nearly sunset by now — they might be back any minute."

Almost as he spoke, the cave started to get lighter and voices floated in from the entrance.

"... No, no, no, A-dog's-nose, it's only at sunset. You can't see the island at all from this side ... Have to know *exactly* where to fly. Anyway, come along in, it's late, we should get some sleep."

A vast green dragon lumbered past them, accompanied by a small bouncy dragon, a girl, a boy, and a duck. A rat was poking his head out of the boy's tunic, twitching his whiskers and making a chittering sound.

"Has anyone been in here while we've been gone?" said the boy. "Ferocious thinks he can smell something, and there's definitely a sense of ... I don't know *what* exactly, but it's definitely familiar ..."

Jerome held his breath. Snotty frowned and scattered another small sprinkling of powder in front of them, just as Great-Aunt Wilhelmina raised her head and sniffed.

"No, I can't smell anything strange," the dragon rumbled. "There's a reek of magic, of course, coming off that potion you're carrying. It might be that you're sensing, Max."

"Maybe," said Max, doubtfully, but there didn't seem to be any other explanation.

"So, will it de-ice the castle?" asked Olivia. "What did she say when she gave it to you?"

The Lady had taken Max off to one side to give him the potion, and then there'd been barely enough time for everyone to throw themselves on Great-Aunt Wilhelmina's back before they had to fly hard into the setting sun.

Max looked at the small carved crystal bottle in his hand. It seemed to almost glow with magic. There was only a small amount of potion inside, but then the Lady had said that five or six drops would be enough to do it. Her spell only had to disable Morgana's magic, then Max himself could unravel his icespell.

"She said it would work," said Max. "I've got

some words to say as well, to get it started. But have we got time to sleep? Don't we need to head off straight away to get there before Morgana?"

"I can't fly when it's dark," boomed Great-Aunt Wilhelmina. "I've got terrible night vision. Ever since I got caught in a thunderstorm a couple of hundred years ago, took a lightning bolt straight to the head."

"Are you coming with us?" asked Olivia, thinking that if it came to a showdown with Morgana, it would be rather wonderful to have Great-Aunt Wilhelmina on their side.

"Of course!" said the dragon. "Can't let A-dripnose be the only representative of the family at such an important moment. Besides, I can fly much faster than any of you. If we leave at first light, I'll have you there before midday."

"That should do it," said Max, thinking. "Morgana must have set out at twilight two days ago, so she'll arrive at twilight tomorrow. We should have plenty of time."

In the corner, Jerome and Snotty exchanged glances. Snotty eased a small square piece of folded parchment out of his tunic, and passed it to Jerome.

"I'm going to see if I can get the spell once Max is asleep," he whispered. "But if I get caught, send this swift to Lady Morgana. She'll have to do the last few miles by broomstick. She needs to get to Camelot before midday!"

***

Max woke with a start. The far end of the cave was just visible in the pale light of dawn, but the others were still sleeping. Great-Aunt Wilhelmina let out a rattling snore and Max wondered if that was what had woken him. Then he saw a dark shadow flit across the narrow cave entrance and disappear out into the morning.

Max sat up. He felt around on the blankets. Then he scrambled up and shouted.

"Hey! Wake up! The potion's gone! Someone's been in and they've stolen the spell! It's gone! Quick — we've got to get after them!"

He ran for the cave entrance, barely registering the others as they leaped up to follow him. He sprinted down the narrow passageway and out onto the beach.

There was no one there.

He pelted along the sand and up onto the path that ran from the cove to the nearest road. There was no one to be seen, but there, in the centre of the muddy path, were the prints of at least two horses, and they led off toward the road, looking like whoever was riding them had galloped off in an extreme hurry.

As Max stood there, Adolphus came galumphing up behind him and the others soon followed. Max turned to Great-Aunt Wilhelmina, who was looking rather cross-eyed after her rapid transition from deep sleep to broad daylight.

"It's Snotty Hogsbottom," he groaned. "I should have known. I thought I'd put him off the trail but he must have found us — and now he's got the potion."

"Well, we must follow him, then, and get it

back," said Great-Aunt Wilhelmina. "And since he seems to have disappeared rather rapidly, we'd better do a direction spell, and then fly."

"Umm ... I'm not sure I can," said Max.

"Of course you can, dear boy," said the great dragon impatiently. "Just try. You have more magic in your fingertips than most people manage to acquire in a lifetime. Get on with it, and then we'll catch up with this Hoggy Snotbottom, and all will be well."

"Snotty Hogsbottom," said Olivia. "Not Hoggy Snotbottom."

"Well, Hotty Bogsnottom, then, or Botty Hotsnoggom or whatever his name is," said Great-Aunt Wilhelmina crossly. "Let's just get after him before it's too late!"

Max thought about a direction spell. He picked up a pointed stone from the ground, held it on the palm of his hand and tried to direct the right magic at it.

The stone whizzed around in circles for a few seconds, and then it turned into an apple pie.

Great-Aunt Wilhelmina snorted, but Olivia took the pie happily.

"Breakfast!" she said, and started to divide it between them.

"Try again, Max," said the dragon.

He picked up another stone and focused. This time he was almost sure he'd got it right, but then the stone flew up into the air and hit him on the nose, before dissolving into a thousand sparkling pieces of dust.

"Urrghh," said Max, trying not to breathe any of them in. "Dungballs! Why can't I get it right? We've got to catch up with them. We've got to!"

"Calm down, dear boy," said Great-Aunt Wilhelmina. "I can fly a lot faster than a horse can gallop. We should be able to catch up with them. But we *must* know where they are going."

Max took a deep breath and closed his eyes. He pictured Snotty on his horse, just as he had seen him a couple of days ago. He pictured the crystal potion bottle, humming with the Lady's magic. He picked up a small stick, placed it in his palm, and let the magic flow into it.

The stick quivered, and shifted, and pointed southwest.

"There!" said Olivia. "Come on! Let's get after him!"

They scrambled on to Great-Aunt Wilhelmina's back and she rose into the air on her powerful dragon wings. They started to hurtle the way the stick was pointing — away from the sea, and in exactly the wrong direction for Camelot.

***

Snotty Hogsbottom was galloping hard, throwing out misdirection spells behind him every few minutes while keeping a sharp eye on the road ahead. He had sent Jerome off in the opposite direction, with strict instructions to send the swift to Lady Morgana. Meanwhile, Snotty wanted to make sure he drew Max and the others as far away from the castle as possible, to give Morgana the best chance of beating them to Camelot.

He splashed though a small stream, and dived into a copse of trees, then doubled back and planted a misdirection spell just next to a low stone wall. Following the wall took him to another cart track, and then a wider road. As he looked back, he could just see a faint speck in the sky heading in his direction. Snotty put his head down and urged his horse on to an even more furious gallop.

***

"Hotty Botsnoggums! Stay exactly where you are!"

Great-Aunt Wilhelmina's booming dragon voice rang out across the clearing where Snotty was standing, panting, next to his exhausted horse. Max and Olivia slipped off the dragon's back and moved out either side of her, slowly approaching Snotty, who was clutching the crystal potion bottle in his right hand. Amazingly, Adolphus had already positioned himself at the other end of the clearing to cut off Snotty's retreat, although it was probably because Ferocious was perched on his head whispering instructions into his ear.

"Come on Snotty, hand it over," said Max, as he approached. "You can't get away, and if you hand it over now, we *won't* tell King Arthur about you."

Snotty laughed, scornfully.

"Won't tell King Arthur? Big deal! He's going to be dead, very soon. And if by some miracle he survives, you won't be telling him anything, because then you'd have to tell him exactly *who* did the spell that iced his entire castle and all his knights!"

Max stopped still. It was a very good point. What *was* he going to tell King Arthur, assuming they got him defrosted?

Snotty saw Max's hesitation and laughed again.

"Well, Pendragon, just realized how genius my lady's plan was? Even if you do save the castle, which you won't, you can't tell anyone about how it happened."

"Oh shut up, Hogsbottom, and hand over the potion!" shouted Olivia, as she launched herself at him. Snotty twisted away, and as he did so, he pulled the stopper out of the potion bottle and upturned it.

Before Olivia could grab it, all the golden liquid inside had splashed out onto the grass.

There was an awful silence as everyone looked at each other, Max and Olivia in horror, Snotty with a smile of triumph as he threw down the empty bottle. Then Max hurled himself at Snotty with both fists out and the two boys tumbled to the ground, rolling over and over across the clearing. Snotty nearly landed a punch on Max's right ear, but Max managed to dodge it, grabbing a fistful of Snotty's hair.

"Ow!" yelled Snotty as Max pulled his head sideways, but the next second he'd got Max in a headlock and was squeezing his throat.

"Urrgh," gurgled Max, as he tried to prise Snotty's arm away from his neck. Then, with a huge effort, Max wrenched himself around and kneed Snotty in the stomach. But the fight would still have gone against Max, if Olivia had not stepped in. She'd been standing over the struggling boys, trying to get a clear angle on Snotty, and Max's blow was just what she needed. Snotty's head went up, and Olivia's fist connected with his ear.

Thud!

For the second time in a few months Snotty Hogsbottom fell back heavily, knocked out cold by a Pendragon.

"Hurrah! Hurrah! You've won!" shouted Adolphus as he bounded up.

But there was no cheering from anyone else. They were all looking at the empty crystal bottle lying on the ground, and wondering what they were going to do now the potion was gone.

A Race to Save Camelot!

Max stared at the potion bottle in despair. Morgana had won. There was nothing they could do. He sat down heavily and put his head on his knees. After a moment, Ferocious scampered over and sniffed all round the neck of the bottle. Then he jumped up on Max's shoulder and nipped his ear.

"Max! Look! There's still a few drops of potion in it!"

They all looked. Ferocious was right — inside the bottle was the tiniest pool of potion, cupped in the curve of the glass.

Hardly daring to breathe, Max picked up the bottle and looked closer. There looked to be about two drops of the golden-coloured spell still there. He looked up at Great-Aunt Wilhelmina, who was peering down at the potion.

"What do you think? Is it enough?"

"Hmmm. I doubt if it will de-ice the whole castle. But it might be enough to do a small portion of it. If we could get the spell directly to where Merlin is . . ." She closed her eyes, and thought. After a few moments, she opened them again.

"Vortigern?"

"Quack!" said the duck. "Right here, my lady. Anything I can do?"

"Did you not tell me, once, that you used to sneak up one of the castle drains to get to the kitchen?"

"Quack! Yes. Good route to get a bit of . . ."

"Genius!" shouted Max. "Because the kitchen

drain also runs under the Great Hall! I know that, because you can sometimes smell the cooking when you're in there!"

"Won't the drains be full of ice?" said Olivia, doubtfully.

"It's quite unlikely," said Great-Aunt Wilhelmina. "Ice around the bounds of the castle above the ground is one thing — icing the earth beneath would need much more power."

Suddenly everyone started to get excited. It looked like it might still be possible to foil Morgana's plot. If they could just get to Merlin and free him from the spell, he could finish the job.

"Come on!" said Great-Aunt Wilhelmina. "No time to lose. That dreadful Hoggy Snotbottom has led us miles out of our way. Climb on my back, and we'll be off."

"What about Snotty?" said Olivia. He appeared to still be completely out cold, but she didn't trust him.

"I'll carry him in my claws," said the dragon.

"Then we can make sure he doesn't get up to any mischief." She grinned, and flexed her great claws, and Max thought he was rather glad not to be Snotty Hogsbottom at that moment.

**

It was an hour past midday when they glided in to land by the gatehouse in front of Camelot. The ice mountain was glittering in the full sunshine, the castle still just a shadow buried behind its smooth blue-white surface. Max had forgotten just how awesomely large the mountain was. He bit his lip, and hoped the small amount of spell they had was up to the job.

As they landed, a figure came striding out of the gatehouse waving his sword, followed by a band of soldiers trying their best to look fierce. As the figure got closer, Max realized it was Sir Lionel, calling out in a firm voice:

"Dragon! Begone! The castle is guarded and we will defend it to the . . . Oh, I say. It's Lady Wilhelmina! And . . . Max! Olivia! Thank goodness you're safe!"

The soldiers looked highly relieved when they realized the enormous green dragon was friendly, and put their swords away. Sir Lionel ran over and clapped Max on the shoulder.

"Good to see you! I was really worried. We had soldiers combing the woods for you and Olivia ... As you can see, we've been caught out by that traitor sorceress — the whole castle's been iced. But Lady Morgana's on her way, thank goodness. In fact, we got a swift just a few hours ago. She's doing the last bit by broomstick, should be here any minute now."

Max and the others looked at each other in horror. Morgana shouldn't have been due till twilight. They had thought they'd have at least three or four hours. Now it looked like they had a matter of minutes.

At that moment, Sir Richard Hogsbottom emerged from the gatehouse, making a great show of strapping on his sword, and calling, "Sorry — bit of trouble with my armour — everything all right here, Lionel?"

Then he saw Snotty.

"Adrian! Adrian, my boy! What happened?"

Snotty had regained consciousness hours before, only to find himself suspended a few hundred feet above the ground, gripped rather painfully in large dragon claws. He had spent the rest of the flight alternately groaning and being sick, and now he was lying on the ground looking like a wet dishcloth. He raised his head feebly.

"Max and the others found a spell to de-ice the castle. I was helping but . . . I dropped the bottle accidentally and it all spilled . . . I'm afraid they weren't very understanding about it." He tried to look both sorrowful and nobly ready to forgive them.

"My dearest boy," said Sir Richard. "How unkind of them. You don't look at all well, I must say."

Great-Aunt Wilhelmina rolled her eyes.

"Are you Sir Richard Hogsbottom?" she enquired of the tubby knight. When he nodded, she looked at him sternly, still keeping one clawed foot firmly on Snotty's stomach. "This boy has made a perfect nuisance of himself, and you need to take better control of him. He nearly destroyed the potion we received from the Lady of the Island. Luckily, there were a few drops left . . ." At these words, Snotty started, and Sir Richard looked rather green. She grinned. "I believe Max was going to have a try at the spell . . . Now, where *is* Max?"

They looked all around, but Max had gone. And so, Olivia realized, had Vortigern.

***

The main castle drain was surprisingly narrow, half full of water, and extremely smelly. Vortigern was splashing happily up ahead, and Max, trying to ignore the old bits of mouldy food and worse that were floating in the scum, was following him rather more gingerly.

As soon as he'd heard how close Morgana was, Max knew he had to do something fast. He'd caught Vortigern's eye, and the pair of them had sneaked off while everyone else was distracted by Sir Richard

Hogsbottom. They'd hurried to the drain outlet by the moat and, once there, Max had decided that the quickest and easiest way to get up the drain was as a frog. He'd tied the precious potion bottle around Vortigern's neck, and had reached for the magic. It had been almost easy this time, thinking his way into the transformation. And now he felt surprisingly comfortable as a frog, splashing through the muddy water.

"Quack!" said Vortigern, and stopped suddenly. "I think this is the one."

Max looked at the small side vent that led upward from the drain.

If it was the right one, it would come out just in front of the huge fireplace in the Great Hall, where it caught the dripping fat and juices from the huge hogs roasted there during feasts. If it was the wrong one, it would quite likely end up in the toilet of some knight's chamber . . .

Max swallowed, and started to hop up the sloping tunnel. He turned to Vortigern.

"You'll have to come, too. You've got the potion bottle."

Vortigern scrambled after him, and together they carefully made their way up toward the strange blueish light coming from the ice at the top of the drain.

"Ow!" Max was brought up short as he hit the wall of ice, blocking any further progress. He peered into the whiteness and tried to make out where they were.

"It is the Great Hall," he said. "It's the right shape — too big for a toilet. But I can't really see anything. We're going to have to clear some space with one drop of the spell, and then see where we are."

Together they eased the bottle open, Vortigern clutching the stopper in his beak while Max pulled the bottle with his froggy hands. Once it was open, he tipped it carefully over, and watched one single precious drop roll down the neck and cling to the lip of the bottle. Max took a deep breath and shook the drop onto the ground. At the same time, he said the words of the spell that the Lady had taught him, and gathered all the magic of his own that he could.

The drop of potion fizzed as it hit the ground, and a vast billowing spout of purple smoke wreathed around Max and Vortigern, swirling upwards into the ice, dissolving it as it went. Max concentrated as hard as he could, unravelling the spell he had cast, pulling it apart bit by bit, willing it to dissolve outwards from the spot where he stood. And it did — he could feel it cracking and crumbling and disappearing into a puff of nothing, further and further . . . Until it felt like he hit a brick wall. Morgana's magic was there again, like a locked door, and the reversal stopped dead.

Max looked at Vortigern. The duck grinned.

"Definitely something. My feathers went quite tingly. Let's go and see."

They scrambled up out of the drain opening, into the Great Hall, and stared around them. The de-icing had cleared almost half of the vast chamber, and there was now plenty of room for Max to move around in.

Unfortunately, the half that was still encased in ice was the half with King Arthur's great council table, and the king and all his knights were seated around it, looking like they were in earnest discussion. They were about twenty feet away from the sheer wall of ice that marked the outer edge of Max's successful reversal.

Only Merlin was not at the table. Merlin, who looked like he was explaining something rather tricky to the assorted knights, had positioned himself where all the men could see him clearly, at some distance from the table. He was only about five feet away from where Max was standing...

Max turned to Vortigern.

"We're nearly there. We just need one more go. But this time, I think I'll be human."

He closed his eyes, and thought his way back into being a boy, barely noticing the whoosh of stars as he transformed. His mind was fixed on the potion, and the spell, and Merlin, and how little time they had left.

Morgana's Spell

Sir Lionel was feeling rather confused. It was not easy being the most senior knight left in the kingdom, and although he had Sir Richard Hogsbottom to help, somehow he didn't feel that Sir Richard was quite as concerned about the situation as he ought to be. There was a certain smugness in his voice and look as he contemplated the iced castle ... And now a powerful dragon had arrived with Sir Bertram's children, claiming they had a potion to reverse the icespell and seeming quite keen to get on with the job before Lady Morgana got here.

Sir Lionel frowned. He'd known Lady Wilhelmina for a long time. She had always been a good friend to the king. And she'd never been too fond of Lady Morgana. He looked at Snotty, lying on the ground with a pained expression, with the dragon's great claw trapping him firmly. Then he looked at Sir Richard, wringing his hands and looking anxious at the news that some of the reversal spell had survived and Max had disappeared with it.

"So. Why not just wait for Lady Morgana?" he asked the huge dragon abruptly. She looked down at him with her amber eyes and considered.

"Because she's an evil, scheming sorceress, Sir Lionel, as you should very well have realized. And she's behind the whole plot."

Olivia gasped, and Sir Richard Hogsbottom

started to stutter, "Now, now, that's quite slanderous, I can't permit such talk ..." but he was silenced by a gesture from Sir Lionel, who was looking up at Great-Aunt Wilhelmina with an odd expression.

"And will you be telling this to the king, if we manage to set him free?"

"Of course not!" snorted Great-Aunt Wilhelmina. "He knows I dislike Morgana. Had a terrible row with him about her marrying Uriel and moving up to Gore. Right on my doorstep! I nearly burned down the castle, I was so cross ... No, he wouldn't believe me. Just call it a grudge. There's no proof — and anyway, he knows she couldn't have done the spell herself, not all the way from Gore. Not possible. So she's completely in the clear."

"And here she comes," observed Ferocious, who had just spotted a dark figure on a broomstick coast in toward the gatehouse and land gracefully a few hundred yards away. Olivia clenched her fists.

"Come on, Max," she muttered. "Come on! Get on with it. She's here!"

***

Max had the potion bottle gripped firmly in his hand, and was trying to peer down the neck to see if there was still a full drop left. It looked like more than half of the tiny remnants of the spell had been used up already. He looked across at the frozen knights. He could see Sir Bertram, caught just as he was twisting up the ends of his magnificent moustache. Next to him, Lancelot had one eyebrow raised, and at the end of the table Arthur was watching Merlin, his blue eyes troubled and his face stern.

Merlin, Max realized, appeared to be concentrating very hard. And as Max looked, he saw a slight drip form on the end of Merlin's nose. Which meant that the ice near him was starting to melt! Somehow, Merlin was fighting the effects of the spell, even from inside the ice.

"Quack!" said Vortigern, looking up at Max. "Get on with it, Max — we might only have a few seconds left!"

***

"So pleased to see you, Lady Wilhelmina," said Morgana, coming up to the dragon with a smile painted on to her white face. Great-Aunt Wilhelmina snorted, and a faint haze of smoke emerged from her nostrils.

Morgana looked around at them all, and noted Snotty, flat out on the ground, and Sir Richard's anxious expression. She smiled graciously at Olivia, but her eyes were cold.

"And where is dear Max?" she said, in her honeyed voice.

Olivia shivered.

"He's gone to ... er ... look for—"

"He's gone to save King Arthur!" said Adolphus, proudly. "He's in the castle, with the potion we got from the Lady! It's a rever ... um ... reverting, er ... reversal spell!"

He looked exceedingly pleased with himself for getting the word right, and flapped his wings happily. Ferocious groaned.

Morgana stood up extremely straight. Her face looked like she'd had a bucket of iced water tipped over her. She looked over at the castle, and then whipped a large green potion bottle out of her robes.

"Just as well I hurried," she said. "There's no knowing what *Max* might do to the castle if he tries to reverse the spell. Probably turn them all into ants!" She laughed, but her laughter was brittle, and her expression was savage. "No time to lose," she said, and held up the potion above her head.

Olivia launched herself at Morgana and knocked her flying. The sorceress landed on top of Snotty, who yelled loudly, and her potion bottle went hurtling through the air, coming to rest on the grass twenty yards away. Sir Richard scuttled after it, but before he could pick it up, Sir Lionel strode over and put his large foot firmly down on top of it.

"Apologies, my lady," he said. "So sorry, young Olivia tripped and stumbled into you. Let me get you your potion."

He picked the bottle up deliberately and

examined it. Then he slowly started to walk toward them. Morgana had picked herself up rapidly, while Snotty lay groaning and clutching his stomach. Olivia was sitting up looking slightly dazed and holding her head, but Ferocious had entered the fray and was biting Morgana's ankles, while she kicked out in a most unladylike fashion and tried to drive him off.

"Hand me that potion!" she shrieked at Sir Lionel. Her hair was flying in all directions and her eyes were full of fury.

He bowed.

"Of course, my lady, of course..."

But before Sir Lionel could delay any further, Snotty, who was just next to him, snatched the potion bottle from his hand and threw it to Morgana. She caught it expertly, and with a triumphant smile, she shook the entire contents out onto the grass, raised her hands and said the words of the spell.

***

In the Great Hall, the last small droplet of the Lady of the Island's spell dripped out of the potion bottle onto the ground and fizzed slightly, a wisp of purple smoke circling up from it. Max felt a lightening of Morgana's connection spell and closed his eyes and pushed with all his strength at the ice-wall in front of him, undoing the magic he'd done, tearing it apart as rapidly as he could, pushing as far into the ice as possible. He felt it give, and melt away, but he wasn't sure if he'd reached Merlin, and he could already feel the effects of the Lady's magic wearing off. Desperately he willed away the ice around Merlin, thinking hard of the wizard's warm voice and hawk-like eyes. There was a faint crack, and Max opened his eyes.

He'd succeeded in driving the ice-wall back, almost completely freeing Merlin, and it seemed the wizard himself was finishing the job. As Max watched, Merlin put out his arms and pushed the ice away from him, and then strode forward, frowning.

"Max! What's happened?" He looked around and

saw the rest of the hall frozen in solid ice, and then turned back to Max, his hand on his sword. "Flame and thunder! Who's responsible for this?"

"I am," said Max hurriedly. "But I'll tell you everything later. Right now Morgana is—"

There was an enormous *BOOM!* that reverberated through the entire castle. Merlin's eyes widened and he flung up his hand, placing a protection spell over them all. As the icespell was ripped away by Morgana's magic, a shockwave from the reversal seemed to shake everything in the castle. Merlin staggered, as if a great weight were pushing at him. Then it was gone, and Merlin straightened. He looked rather grey, but he appeared to be all right. All around the hall, knights were stirring, as the effects of the icespell wore off and they found themselves suddenly awake and wondering what on earth had just happened.

***

Olivia and the others watched in awe as the ice mountain cracked from top to bottom then started to shatter into tiny pieces. The fragments sparkled in the sun and then vanished as if they had never existed.

Lady Morgana clapped her hands together and took a deep breath.

"Well, Sir Lionel," she said, her voice quite restored to its usual warm honeyed tones. "You see — I managed to reverse the spell before Max could do any irreparable damage! I'm afraid we may not find many people *alive* in there, but let's hope *very* hard that one of them is my dear brother . . ."

She smiled in satisfaction. Olivia felt sick, and she noticed that Sir Lionel was also looking rather pale. But Sir Richard Hogsbottom looked like someone had just handed him a gold chain of office, and Snotty had a smile of triumph.

Suddenly Great-Aunt Wilhelmina let out a roar and a spout of blue-white flame.

"Your luck's in, Morgana!" she boomed. "I can see the king . . . and Merlin . . . and Max!"

She was right. Striding across the drawbridge, sword at the ready, was King Arthur, with Merlin by his side and all his knights following. Alongside Merlin was Max, looking exhausted, and waddling next to him was a small but very pleased-looking duck.

"Hurrah! Hurrah!" shouted Adolphus, bouncing up and down, and Ferocious scampered up onto the top of the small dragon's head where he could get a better view. Olivia felt a huge wave of relief as she watched Max walking toward them, and she joyfully punched Sir Lionel on the arm.

"He did it! Max saved them!"

"Well, technically it was Lady Morgana who de-iced the castle," observed Sir Lionel with a grin. "But I rather think you're right — I think Max may very well have saved them." With a slight nod of his head he indicated the place where Lady Morgana had just been standing. When she had seen the figures emerging from the castle, she had crumpled to the ground in a dead faint.

The Swordspell

It was dark by the time the castle got back to any semblance of normality. Arthur had rushed around checking the defences, while getting reports from Sir Lionel and Sir Richard on all that had happened while he had been trapped in the ice. Lady Morgana had been revived and taken to the chambers she usually occupied in Camelot, and her retinue had arrived from Gore. It seemed she would now be staying until the Festival of Chivalry in three weeks' time.

"She wore herself out with that reversal spell, Merlin," said Arthur as they finally sat down to supper. "As well as hardly sleeping, so she could get down here from Gore as quickly as she did. We owe her our lives." He looked solemnly at the wizard. "I know you have had your doubts about Morgana, but really, this time there's proof. She couldn't have had anything to do with it — and she broke the icespell to save us. What more do you want?"

Merlin grimaced. "My lord, it is indeed clear that Lady Morgana cannot have cast the icespell herself. It is impossible to cast a spell so powerful from such a great distance. We shall obviously have to keep looking for this other sorceress, and hope we find her soon." He sighed. "However, I must urge you to treat Lady Morgana with some caution — I have been talking to Sir Lionel, and—"

King Arthur held up his hand for silence, and looked sternly at Merlin, his blue eyes bright. "I

147

won't talk about it, Merlin, I'm sorry. I had Sir Lionel approach me, too, but what he said didn't amount to any kind of proof of anything, and I won't have it repeated." He suddenly looked weary, and rubbed his face with his hands. "She is my *sister*," he said, in a low voice, "and I trust her. There's the beginning and the end of it all."

***

"So, it looks like she's gotten away with it again," said Lancelot the next morning, as they all strolled across the grass to see off Great-Aunt Wilhelmina. "The king is overjoyed that events have finally put paid to any hint of suspicion of Morgana, and won't hear another word against her. And we have no proof, unfortunately."

"Yes, very unfortunately," said Merlin, looking at Max sternly. "If you hadn't allowed yourself to get tricked into a most unwise display of power, we might not have—"

"Oh now, Merlin, enough of that!" boomed Great-Aunt Wilhelmina. "Leave the poor boy alone, or I might have to recount the tale of how you brought a certain king's new castle down around his ears when you were just a slip of a lad!"

Max looked up at Great-Aunt Wilhelmina in surprise, and she winked at him with one golden eye.

"Seem to recall you had to invent some gobbledegook about dragons being responsible," she said, looking very hard at Merlin, while the corner of her mouth twitched.

Merlin coloured and coughed.

"Well, yes, er ... you're right, of course, Lady Wilhelmina. We all make mistakes when young. Perhaps best not to dwell on these things ..."

Lancelot laughed. "You brought a whole castle down? I'm not sure I've heard about that one. I should write a song about it!"

Merlin looked a bit uncomfortable, but then grinned. "Well, yes. Actually it was rather spectacular. No one inside, of course, it had only just been built. Anyway — that's a story for another day ..." He turned to Great-Aunt Wilhelmina. "We're extremely grateful to you, my lady. And please — send my love and thanks to the Lady of the Island when you next see her."

"Will do, Merlin, will do," the dragon rumbled. "Well, now — good luck to all of you! I'm sure you'll sort Morgana out eventually. She can't get away with it forever. Be good, A-doll's-house! And find some way to get even with that dreadful Botty Hogsnottom!"

And with a few more final farewells to them all, she launched herself into the air and was soon just a flash of green heading rapidly west.

Merlin and Lancelot had duties in the castle, but the rest of them decided to head to the river for the afternoon. Max and Olivia had made a point, the day before, of seeking out Fred the kitchen boy. They had made him a present of the rather nice skinning knife Max had received for Christmas. Fred was surprised, but very grateful, and had sneaked them a whole sack of fresh pastries from the buttery that morning to say thank you.

"You know," said Max, as they stretched out by the pool in the sunshine and picked at the last pastry crumbs, "I thought I'd get a lot worse telling off from Merlin. Three cheers for Great-Aunt Wilhelmina, eh? Still, I'm going to keep my head down for a bit. I'm quite looking forward to the Festival of Chivalry — for once I'm the one that can sit back and watch, and you'll be the one everyone will be looking at!"

Olivia made a face. "Looking at me make a total fool of myself, you mean."

"No! You're very good. Honest. I think you might even win. If someone turns Mordred into a caterpillar before the contest ..."

Olivia brightened. "Hey — Max! I don't suppose ... ?"

"No, sorry, no way. Merlin would smell the magic a mile off, and I'm in enough trouble for the icespell. But you never know — he might break a leg in training or something ..."

"I wish," muttered Olivia, thinking of red-haired Mordred flat on his back on a stretcher.

"Of course, Lady Morgana will be cheering him on, since he's her nephew," observed Ferocious. "Be good if you could beat him to a pulp, really."

"Quack!" said Vortigern, suddenly emerging noisily from the water. "Yes! One of your great punches straight to the left ear!"

"Hey, Vortigern!" exclaimed Max, happily. "Where did you come from?"

"Been catching up with my cousin Guido," said Vortigern. "Three castle servants in his duckpond already, and she's only been here one day. Quite a witch, that Morgana le Fay, eh?"

"She's an evil old hag," said Olivia. "But she seems to have a knack of getting away with it."

"Maybe not this time," said Vortigern, bobbing his head. "With this swordspell idea."

Max raised his head. "Swordspell? What do you mean?"

"Quack!" said Vortigern. "I was in the duckpond with Guido, chasing some of the castle goldfish, and who should go past but Morgana, with Sir Richard and that awful Snotty. Thought I'd waddle after them, see what they were up to . . ."

He dived under the water again, and came up with a bob of his head, splashing water over everyone.

"Vortigern!" said Olivia. "What did you hear?"

"Quack!" said the duck, with a twinkle in his beady eye. "Got any bread?"

Max laughed. "Of course! But not till *after* you've told us what they said!"

"Fair enough," said Vortigern, and waddled closer, lowering his voice. "They said that it would have to be the swordspell now. It was the last chance. The swordspell would do for Arthur good and proper. They only had to wait another three weeks and Morgana would be queen. So. How about the bread?"

Max threw a piece into the river and turned to the others.

"What on earth does that mean?"

"It means," said Ferocious, "that we've got another chance to catch Morgana out. We can show the king that she really is behind all this trickery. We can save the kingdom from her forever!"

"Yes, yes!" said Adolphus enthusiastically. "We'll do it! We'll save them all!"

Olivia looked thoughtful. "They're planning something for the Festival of Chivalry. That's why it's three weeks' time. We just have to find out what."

They looked at each other solemnly.

"Right," said Max. "That's it. Morgana's got away with it three times now. This time we're going to catch her at it. We're going to find out all about her swordspell plot, and prove to the king that she really is an evil, treacherous witch."

"Hurrah for us!" said Adolphus, and gave an extra big bounce, losing his balance. His tail swept sideways as he fell, knocking Olivia flying into Max, and all three of them slipped, flailing, off the grassy bank and splashed into the river.

"Nice one, Adolphus," said Ferocious, grinning, as he watched them emerge dripping and staggering from the water. "With your brains, Max's sense of balance and Olivia's tact and ladylike qualities, we're truly a team to be reckoned with. Morgana won't know what's hit her."

Max shook the worst of the water off and stretched out again on the grass. It was a lovely afternoon, and the sun would dry them off soon enough. He closed his eyes and listened to the birds chirruping in the trees behind him, the insects droning past and the rustle of the water in the slight breeze.

He had let himself get caught out by Snotty over the icespell, but he was not going to let that happen again. He was going to prove to Merlin that he could be a seriously great wizard. If it took every ounce of his magic, he was going to find out about Morgana's swordspell and stop her once and for all.

About the author

C. J. Busby lived on boats until she was sixteen, and remembers one terrifying crossing of the English Channel in gale-force winds, when her family's barge nearly overturned.

She spent most of her childhood with her nose in a book, even when walking along the road. Luckily she survived to grow up, but she still carried on reading whenever she could. After studying science at university, she lived in a South Indian fishing village and did research for her PhD.

She currently lives in Devon, England, with her three children, and she borrows their books whenever they let her.

Don't miss Max and Olivia's first hilarious adventures!

And, coming soon, the thrilling conclusion . . .

Max and Olivia have discovered that Morgana le Fay is plotting to use a mysterious swordspell against King Arthur at the Festival of Chivalry. They don't know what the spell is or how to stop it, and Olivia also has her training for the Squire's Challenge to worry about.

But things are made even worse when Merlin is called away unexpectedly, leaving Max and Olivia without his magical protection. With the help of Sir Lancelot, Sir Bertram, Adolphus, Ferocious and Vortigern, the Pendragon children must quickly uncover Morgana's evil plan, before it is too late for Arthur and Camelot!